CONTENTS

RAMOSE: PRINCE IN EXILE

RAMOSE AND THE TOMB ROBBERS

RAMOSE

PRINCE IN EXILE

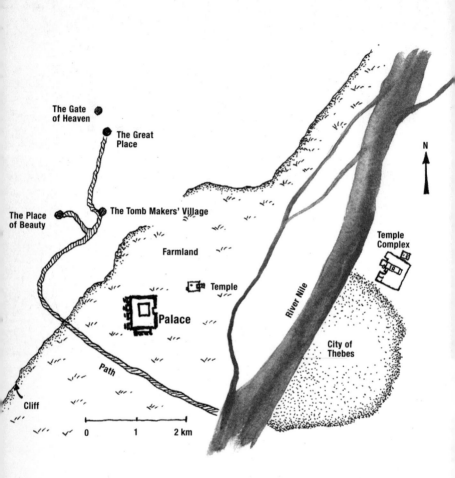

The Gate
of Heaven

The Great
Place

The Place
of Beauty

The Tomb Makers' Village

Farmland

Temple

Palace

Path

Cliff

N

Temple
Complex

River Nile

City of
Thebes

0   1   2 km

PHARAOH'S HEIR

THE BOY was standing on a dry, rocky hill. He looked around. There wasn't a blade of anything growing. He looked down at himself. Why were his clothes so dusty and why was he wearing such awful reed sandals? Where were his red leather ones with the turned-up toes? He heard a mournful chanting drifting up from below. Snaking along in the valley was a *procession. At the front was a jackal-headed priest. The sun reflected on gold and jewels. A beautiful coffin on an ornate sled was being pulled by six oxen. Six priests followed behind. They all wore brilliant white robes with leopard skins draped over their shoulders.*

It was a funeral procession. The boy looked closer. How many loads of funeral goods were there? How many mourners were there?

He had a special interest in this funeral.

It was his own.

Ramose awoke and shivered. He hoped it was a dream, but he was too scared to open his eyes. What if it wasn't? He opened one eye. He could see something green. He opened the other eye. He could see something blue. He sighed with relief. He was in his sleeping chamber. Above him was the bright coloured wall painting of his father hunting a hippopotamus. His father was standing on a papyrus boat about to throw a spear. The river beneath the boat teemed with fish and eels. The unfortunate hippopotamus, unaware of his fate, wallowed in the mud at the water's edge. The reeds growing on the river bank were full of birds and butterflies. On the other wall was a painting of the blue-skinned god Amun.

Ramose had woken up to these paintings all his life and he loved them. He didn't see his father very often in the flesh, but he had the painting to look at, and Amun, king of the gods, was always there watching over him while he slept.

Through the window Ramose could see the date palms and tamarisk trees in his own private courtyard. He got up from his bed and walked outside. The air was already warm even though it was early. He climbed up the stone stairs to the roof. The white-walled palace buildings spread in front of him.

Ramose breathed in deeply. A familiar smell filled his nostrils, the damp, slightly rotting smell of the fields to the east where all the palace food was grown. Beyond the palace walls, beyond the gardens, was the silver, glittering strip of the Nile. On the other side of the river was the sprawling city of Thebes and, to the north, the temple complex with towering obelisks and colourful pennants fluttering from gold-tipped flagpoles.

Ramose climbed back down again. Two servants were waiting to dress him in a clean white kilt and a tunic—both made of fine linen. They brought him fresh bread, sweet cake filled with dried plums and pomegranate juice for his breakfast. He sat down on an elegant chair with legs that ended in carved lion's feet. He chewed on the bread while the servants put on his sandals.

"Not those," he said kicking away the brown sandals the servant was putting on his feet.

"I want the red leather ones with the turned-up toes."

One of the servants spilt a few drops of juice on the floor.

"You're a clumsy fool," said Ramose crossly. "And this bread is too hard. Tell the baker I like it softer."

Heria came in with Topi, his pet monkey. The animal screeched, ran over and snatched the bread from his mouth. Ramose laughed.

"I dreamt I was watching my own funeral procession, Heria." Ramose's smile faded as he remembered his dream again. "What does that mean?" Heria was the royal children's nanny. She had also been their father's nanny. She was now an old woman with greying hair. Heria knew all about dreams.

"Dreaming of your own death is a good omen," said the old woman fiddling with the small flask-shaped amulet she always wore around her neck. "It means you will have long life." She smiled fondly at the boy.

Ramose was relieved. Heria had once kept him away from the river for a month because he'd dreamt that he was drinking a cup of green water. She'd thought that was a very bad dream that meant he would die from drowning.

"Haven't you finished yet?" Ramose snapped at the servant who was combing his hair. He pushed the servant away roughly and took Topi in his arms. The monkey wrapped its tail around Ramose's arm like a furry bracelet.

Ramose went out into the corridor. He was in the mood for a game. He entered the western hall. It contained nothing but six enormous stone columns made of red granite brought all the way from Kush. They were so big that three men clasping hands wouldn't have been able to reach around one of them. The columns reached high above him, higher than the palm trees. Their tops were decorated to look like giant papyrus reeds, but painted bright colours: red, blue and yellow. Ramose didn't feel dwarfed by the giant columns. He'd been walking beneath them all his life.

The palace was a lonely place these days. His father was away on a campaign in Kush, or was it Punt? Ramose's father was away on campaigns most of the time and Ramose often forgot exactly where he was. And his brothers. His brothers were gone.

Wadzmose, his elder brother had died in a chariot accident three years ago while he was doing military service in Memphis, the city in the north of Egypt. Amenmose, who had been only a year older than Ramose, had got some sort of stomach sickness after eating stuffed ibex and had died the year before. His mother was only a distant memory. Now there was only him and his sister, Hatshepsut. Apart from Tuthmosis of course, his snivelling little half-brother and the brat's ugly mother, Mutnofret. They kept to their own part of the palace, thank Amun. Hopefully they'd soon be going to the women's palace at Abu Ghurob for the winter months.

The only people he passed in the hall were servants. They all looked down as they passed him. They weren't allowed to look into his eyes. He liked to turn towards them quickly, so that he could catch them out. If they did look him in the eye, they had to get down on their knees and beg his forgiveness.

He came to his sister's apartments. She was still in her robing room.

"Come and play with me, Penu," he called out to his sister, using the nickname he called her by, which meant "mouse".

"I'm too old for games," she replied from the depths of her rooms. "Go and play with your silly monkey."

Ramose was about to go in and pull her hair, but one of his sister's companions stopped him.

"You can't go into your sister's chamber," she said.

Ramose didn't argue. His sister's companions were sterner than the guards. They weren't servants, but daughters of his father's officials and they treated Hatshepsut as if she was a delicate vase that would easily break. He left his sister's rooms.

By the time he reached the eastern hall, Ramose would have welcomed any company, anyone to talk to—anyone except Vizier Wersu whom he saw walking towards him. Ramose quickly ducked behind a column. Wersu was the most important man in Egypt after the pharaoh. Ramose didn't like him. He was tall and thin with bony hands that felt like large insects when they touched you. He had a thin-lipped mouth full of small sharp teeth. The vizier reminded Ramose of a crocodile. He usually sat quietly in the background, but he could turn dangerous at the blink of an eye.

"Good morning," said a deep, growling voice. Ramose jumped. Wersu had come up behind him. Ramose sometimes thought the vizier had eyes that could see through stone. "I hope Your Highness had a restful night."

His thin mouth smiled, but his eyes held a different message. They told Ramose that the vizier didn't really wish that he'd had a restful night at all. It was almost as if he knew about his nightmare. Topi growled. He didn't like Wersu either.

"I slept extremely well, Vizier. I'm most refreshed."

Ramose continued down the corridor and out into the garden. He sat by the lotus pool while Topi ran up the palm trees to get dates. Remembering his dream had made Ramose feel uneasy. Keneben, Ramose's tutor, came into the garden. He was a young man with a pleasant face that was usually smiling.

"It's time for your lessons, Highness," he said bowing to the boy.

Ramose liked his tutor a lot, but that didn't mean that he liked his lessons.

"I'm not doing any lessons today," Ramose said, folding his arms crossly. "I want to go down to the river to fish instead."

"Your lessons are very important, Prince Ramose," said Keneben patiently.

"Why? They're dull."

"Pharaoh's heir must be wise."

Ramose still wasn't used to the idea that he would be pharaoh one day. When he was young it had always been his brothers who had to shoulder that burden. He had been free to play with the other palace boys, the sons of his father's officials. Now that both his brothers were dead, the burden was his.

"I don't need to be able to read and write. I just need to learn to hunt and command an army like my father," Ramose complained. "You know I'll have hundreds of scribes to do all the reading and writing for me."

"It would never do for your scribes to be more

knowledgeable than you, Highness," Keneben replied. "Even the vizier should not be more scholarly than the pharaoh."

Ramose didn't mind about the scribes, but he definitely wanted to be smarter than Wersu. Keneben knew he'd won the argument. He smiled and walked towards the schoolroom. Ramose followed him.

THE SCHOOLROOM

PRINCE RAMOSE was a clever boy. He could read the hieroglyphs that were only used for writing on the walls of tombs and temples. He could also read the cursive handwriting that the scribes used for keeping records. He could add up numbers in his head without writing them down. The prince also had a good knowledge of the history of Egypt. He knew the names of all the pharaohs going back to the beginning of time.

There was one thing Ramose wasn't good at though and that was writing. He knew all the words, but when he wrote them down on a papyrus, no one could read them. His writing was untidy and the lines of script wandered up and down the scroll, like beetle trails in the sand. He could never get the right amount of ink on his reed pen. There was either too much and the letters merged into fat inky blobs or there wasn't enough and they were thin and too pale to read. Keneben tried to encourage him to practise every day.

Ramose sat on the floor with his kilt stretched over his crossed knees to make a writing surface. Princess Hatshepsut came into the schoolroom followed by two of her companions. Ramose smiled at his sister. She didn't sit on a reed mat on the floor. She took her place on a chair carved with lotuses, straightening her dress around her and arranging her long hair until she looked like one of the goddesses painted on the temple walls. She was only thirteen years old, just two years older than Ramose and still with a girlish face, but her manner was like that of a grown woman. She moved so gracefully, spoke so quietly and never wanted to do anything silly.

"Why do you come to the schoolroom every day,

Penu?" he asked his sister. "Girls don't have to learn to read and write. If I didn't have to learn, I'd be out doing something more interesting."

"I think it's important to learn the scribal skills," said Hatshepsut taking her pens and palette from her servant. "I will be married one day and my husband will be pleased to have a wife who can help him with his business affairs."

Keneben gave them both a well-worn papyrus to copy.

"Not this one again!" grumbled Ramose. "I've written this out at least fifty times."

It was a text about the benefits of being a scribe, how easy the work was compared to being a farmer or a labourer, how a scribe didn't get calluses on his hands.

Ramose was still grumbling. "I'm never going to be a scribe. What do I care whether they have to work hard or not?"

Hatshepsut didn't complain.

Ramose opened his brush container. It was made of carved ebony with a pattern inlaid in gold, ivory and turquoise. He pulled out a reed and chewed the end to make a brush. He spat out threads of reed. It was a disagreeable thing to have to do. His sister got her servants to prepare her brushes. He'd have to remember to do the same. Keneben brought him a bowl of water. Ramose dipped his brush into the water and then rubbed it on the ink block on his palette. He started to write.

"Wait, Highness!" said Keneben. "First you must say a prayer to Thoth, god of writing, and sprinkle water in offering to him."

"That's what scribes have to do," complained Ramose. "I'm not a scribe."

Hatshepsut was muttering the prayer and sprinkling a few drops of water on her papyrus. She started to copy out the lesson. She wrote in beautiful even script, in perfect arrow-straight lines. Ramose dipped his fingers in the water and dripped too much water on his scroll. He wiped it off with his kilt and started writing.

After they had both copied the text, Keneben dipped his reed pen into his red ink ready to correct their work. On Ramose's papyrus, he crossed out words on every line, rewriting them in red in the margin.

"There is some improvement, Highness." Ramose knew Keneben was lying. "Perhaps you might like to write out some of the words again."

He was only a tutor and he couldn't actually tell the future pharaoh that he had terrible handwriting. Keneben turned to Hatshepsut's papyrus. His red pen hung above her scroll as he read it.

"Not a single mistake, Princess," he said putting down his pen unused. "And every word is perfectly formed as always. Your writing is beautiful to behold."

Hatshepsut smiled at the tutor and he bowed to her as if she was the one complimenting him.

Ramose yawned. "I'm bored with lessons."

"You haven't practised reading hieroglyphs yet, Highness," said Keneben.

Ramose groaned as Keneben unrolled a scroll that was at least five cubits long and covered in word-pictures.

"The hieroglyphs are beautifully drawn, Keneben," Hatshepsut said.

Keneben blushed. "You are very kind, Princess."

"I'll begin reading the scroll," she said.

The text was about a battle fought by a pharaoh from an earlier dynasty. Hatshepsut read well and Ramose was soon following the story and wanting to have a turn at reading.

"It's a lot more interesting than the text about scribes," he said.

Eventually though, Ramose got bored with that as well. He uncrossed his stiff legs and stood up. He had ink spots on his kilt.

"I've had enough lessons. I'm going down to the river to play at naval battles. Do you want to come, Penu?"

His sister laughed. "I'd have skin as dark as a peasant girl's if I went outside as often as you want me to," she said. "I prefer to stay indoors."

A few years ago she would have been as keen as Ramose to pretend the ibis were enemy soldiers and throw papyrus stalk spears at them. Now she thought Ramose's games were childish. She spent all of her time with her women companions who rubbed her pale skin with perfumed oils, tied ornaments in her hair and painted her eyelids green.

Ramose walked quickly along the path that led to the river. Three servants hurried after him. One had a fan to cool the prince if he got hot. Another carried a chair, in case he felt like sitting down. Another brought a water jar and some grapes. Ramose made one of them get into the river and pretend he was a hippopotamus so that he had something to hunt. The servant did as he was told, even though crocodiles had occasionally been seen in that part of the river.

Ramose was bored with the game after ten minutes. Not so long ago, games like that had occupied him for hours. He sank down on the lion-footed chair and sighed. Games weren't any fun when you played alone. Or else he was just getting too old for games. The thought depressed him. He stood up to throw grapes at a passing flock of ducks and slipped in the soft mud at the river's edge. Now there were mud stains as well as ink spots on his kilt. He thought he saw one of the servants smirk to himself. Ramose felt a flash of anger.

"I'm tired," he said. "You can carry me back to the palace."

Two of the servants lifted him on the chair and carried him along the path. He made them go the long way, through the pomegranate grove and around the vegetable gardens. That would teach them to laugh at him.

Heria was waiting for him when they returned to the palace.

"It's past time for your midday meal, Prince," she said. Ramose realised that he was very hungry. He took the old woman's hand. "I feel like a pelican egg, Heria," he said.

"I'll send to the kitchens for one immediately."

Heria and Keneben sat on reed mats on the floor. They would only eat when their prince had finished. Ramose sat down on a stool. A servant girl placed plates of food next to him on a low table.

"I'll have a little gazelle meat and bread while I wait for the pelican egg," he said. Heria held the plates up to him. He picked up the food with his fingers.

"Where's Topi?" he said raising the meat to his mouth.

Heria suddenly screamed. Keneben leapt to his feet and launched himself at Ramose. He slapped

the boy's hand away from his mouth just as he
was about to eat the gazelle meat.

Ramose looked at his tutor in amazement.
"What do you think you're doing?" he demanded
angrily.

Heria was trembling. Her bony finger was
pointing at a lump on the floor. Ramose looked
closer. The lump was brown and furry. It was
Topi. The boy fell to his knees next to his pet.

"What's wrong with him?" He picked up the
animal's limp body. The monkey's tongue was
lolling out of its mouth. "He's dead. Topi's dead."

He looked around at his tutor and his nanny
for explanation. They were both grim faced.
Heria took the amulet from around her neck
and handed it to Keneben. He broke a seal from
the top. The amulet was actually a small flask.
Keneben grabbed hold of Ramose roughly.

"What are you doing? I'll call the guards!"

The tutor's mouth was severe. He didn't answer.
His eyes had a fierce determined look that Ramose
didn't recognise. Ramose was afraid—afraid for
his life. Keneben forced the neck of the flask to
Ramose's lips and tipped the contents into his
mouth. He grabbed the boy's hair and pulled his
head back so that he had no choice but to swallow.
Ramose was surprised at the strength in his
tutor's hands. He felt the bitter-tasting liquid run
down his throat. He broke out of Keneben's hold

and got to his feet. Ramose's legs felt strange. They crumpled beneath him. The room was spinning. Heria was wailing. He could hear the birds in the courtyard calling. The sounds grew further and further away. The faces of his tutor and his nanny grew smaller. He opened his mouth to ask them what they had done to him. Then the floor came up and slapped him in the face.

3

AFTERLIFE

RAMOSE AWOKE and shivered. He hoped it was a dream, but he was too scared to open his eyes. What if it wasn't? He opened one eye. He could see nothing. He felt like he wanted to be sick. He opened the other eye. Everything was still black. He couldn't see a thing, but he could smell something. The salty smell of natron, the stuff that the priests used to preserve bodies before they were mummified. There was also the sharp, sweet smell of juniper oil which was poured over the body after it was wrapped in linen strips. He was lying on a cold stone table. This is no dream, thought Ramose. His stomach turned somersaults. I'm dead. Someone is about to cut open my body, take out my insides and turn me into a mummy. Ramose heard someone moving. He raised his head. There was a figure in the corner leaning over a lamp.

"You're awake!" said a familiar voice.

"Heria!" said Ramose. "Did you die too?"

"You're not dead, Highness."

"But this is a tomb isn't it?"

Heria shook her head, helped Ramose to sit up and gave him some cool water to drink.

"This is an embalming room beneath the temple of Maat," said the old woman.

Ramose was confused. His mind was still foggy. He was lying on the stone table made especially for embalming dead people. He could see the channels that were meant to carry away the blood when the dead bodies were cut open with a sharp flint. What am I doing in an embalming room if I'm not dead, thought Ramose. He drank the water and then immediately vomited it up again. Heria stroked his back the way she always did when he was sick.

"What's happened to me, Heria?"

Ramose was trying to remember what had happened. Something frightening, something so bad his brain was keeping it hidden from him.

Keneben came into the room and bowed to the prince.

"I hope you're feeling better, Highness," he said.

Ramose suddenly remembered the tutor's strong grip and the taste of the bitter liquid. He looked from his tutor to his nanny. The two people he had trusted most in the world.

"You poisoned me," he said, trying to get to his feet.

Keneben knelt at the prince's feet. "No, Highness, I wish you nothing but health and long life."

"Someone tried to poison you, my prince, but they failed, thank Amun."

Heria sat next to Ramose and started to tell him a story. She had told him many stories in his life, but never one that scared him like this one.

"As soon as Queen Mutnofret came to the palace I knew she was trouble," the nanny said. "I never liked her. When your dear mother died Mutnofret made sure that she became Pharaoh's favourite wife. Then your half-brother was born and I guessed what her plan was. She wanted her own son to be the next pharaoh. I found a written spell in an amulet around her brat's neck. I took the spell to Keneben to find out what it meant."

Keneben continued the story. "It was a spell to bring death to you and your royal brothers, Highness. I don't believe peasant magic can kill a royal heir, but when your brother Prince Wadzmose died, I wondered if it really was an accident. When Prince Amenmose died as well, I was convinced that someone was killing the princes and that you would be next."

"Since then, we have watched you day and night," Heria said with tears in her eyes. "Poisoning was what we feared most. That's why we tested all your food on the monkey first."

All the inexplicable things started to make sense.

"Poor Topi," said Ramose. In many ways the monkey had been his best friend.

Ramose took another sip of water. This time it stayed down. Then he tried a mouthful of bread.

"When can I go back to the palace? We must send messengers to my father."

"I don't think that's wise, Highness."

"Why not? If Pharaoh knows what she's done, he'll imprison Queen Mutnofret."

"We can't prove it was her. She'll just deny it. Pharaoh is very fond of her and she has a way of making things sound convincing."

Ramose's head ached. He was finding it difficult to understand what his tutor and nanny were planning.

"But what am I to do? I can't stay here—unless you think I should become an embalmer." Ramose laughed despite the pain in his head and his somersaulting stomach. The idea of him having to work for a living was ridiculous. Keneben and Heria didn't laugh though. They didn't even smile.

"If you're to become pharaoh, Highness, you must stay hidden until you are old enough to claim the throne."

"Hidden? You mean imprisoned?"

"No, Highness."

"We have given this a lot of thought. There are so few people in the palace whom we can really trust. The vizier is more than likely on the side of the queen. He is a powerful man who no one dares to defy. Every servant and slave will be a potential enemy. It's too dangerous for you to stay in the palace."

"We could hide you somewhere in a different town—even a different country."

Ramose shuddered at the thought of leaving Egypt.

"Wherever you go, eventually word will get back to the vizier and the queen."

"The only way that you will be safe is if everyone thinks you're dead."

"The potion you drank, Highness, gave you every appearance of being dead."

Heria wept again at the memory. "When you were taken away for embalming, I managed to switch your body with that of a peasant boy about your age who had just died of an illness."

"Does my father think I am dead? My sister?"

"Yes. It was the only way to ensure your safety."

"But surely you don't expect me to stay here?" Ramose said, indicating the dusty, smelly room.

"No, Highness, of course not," said Keneben. "What I have in mind is that you disguise yourself as an apprentice scribe."

"An apprentice scribe!"

"Yes, Highness," said Heria. "You won't need to do physical work, and you have the scribal skills."

"I have found a scribe looking for an apprentice. He and his wife have no children. They are looking for a boy to train to take the scribe's place."

"I won't become a scribe," shouted Ramose. "I'm Pharaoh's son, the heir to the throne of Egypt. I won't do it. You can't make me!"

4

THE EDGE OF
THE WORLD

RAMOSE LEANED over the side of the papyrus boat and trailed his hand in the blue river water. An old man was rowing the boat across the Nile, the life-blood of Egypt. Without the river Egypt would not exist, he knew that. The river gave Egyptians water to drink and to make their crops grow. Each year in the season of akhet the river turned green and flooded. The fields disappeared beneath its waters. When the water receded and the Nile shrank back to its normal size, a layer of black silt was left over all the farmland. It was a gift from the gods that made fruit and vegetables grow fat and full of flavour.

Ramose knew these things because Keneben had taught him. He cupped some of the Nile water in his hand and drank it.

The small boat reached the western bank of the river and Ramose climbed out. He was wearing a coarse tunic over his kilt. He still had his favourite red leather sandals though. He had insisted on keeping them.

The path from the river skirted around the palace. Behind those walls, which were almost close enough to touch, were his sister, his tutor and his dear nanny. Maybe his father was also there, just returned from a triumphant campaign in Kush. But as well as the people who loved him, there were also people who wished him dead—the queen, the vizier and the brat-prince, Tuthmosis.

Ramose walked on without stopping. There was no one to farewell him as he walked away from the places that were familiar to him. The day before, Heria and Keneben had sneaked away from the palace at different times to say goodbye to him. It was too risky for him to be seen with either of them and they didn't trust anyone to guide him.

Instead, Keneben had drawn a map for the prince on a small sheet of papyrus.

Ramose walked along a path between a canal and fields of wheat and vegetables. The path was shaded by date palms. Peasant farmers went about their daily business without even glancing at him. The path zigzagged past fig trees and grape vines. A man lifted water from a canal and poured it into his fields using a device with a leather bucket at the end of a counter-balanced pole. He carefully watered each melon vine and every onion plant. Ramose breathed in the moist air laden with the heavy smell of ripe fruit, lotus flowers and animal dung.

Then the fields ended abruptly as if someone had drawn a line in the earth. There were no more irrigation canals. The desert began just as suddenly as the fields had ended. And the path immediately changed from a smooth, well-travelled roadway to a rough, sandy track with no trees to shade it. The familiar smells of the Egypt he knew faded and the hot, dry smell-less air of the desert filled his nostrils.

Ramose had never walked in the desert before. It was a dangerous place, inhabited only by barbarians, sand dwellers and the dead. The path started to climb. On either side there was nothing but hot sand—apart from the rock that Ramose managed to fall headlong over. He picked up the rock and threw it angrily down the cliff. It skipped and bounced down the rock face. If Ramose had been in the palace he would have blamed a servant for leaving something in his way for him to fall over. He would have yelled abuse at the servant and that would have made him feel better. Ramose watched the rock smash into a dozen pieces when it hit the bottom. It made him feel worse.

Ramose sat in the sand and had to concentrate hard to stop himself from crying. Normally if he so much as knocked his knee against a stool, three servants would have been at his side to see if he needed attention. A priest would have been called to say a prayer for him. There he was, sprawled in the dirt and no one came to help him. He was alone for the first time in his life. The harsh sun burned the back of his neck. Ramose looked up at the path that rose steeply in front of him. He got to his feet and walked on. He had a long way to go.

The hill turned into a steep cliff and the path zigzagged back and forth sharply in order to find a way up. Jagged stones dug into his sandals as he climbed. Ramose adjusted the bag on his shoulder. It was a small bag made of woven reeds—the sort that peasants carried their food to the fields in. Yet at that moment the simple bag contained all Ramose's possessions.

He reached the top of the cliff and sat down panting. He looked back the way he had come, shading his eyes from the sun. In the distance, he could see the glittering ribbon of the Nile with a stripe of green on each side. He was shocked to see what a thin strip of fertility Egypt was, clinging to the edges of the Nile. The hostile desert beyond stretched as far as the eye could see on either side of it. At the river's edge, he could just make out the whitewashed walls of the palace. On the other side was the sprawling city and the temple complex with its flags flying and its gold glinting in the sunlight. That was where he had spent the last two weeks, hidden in a basement room. He turned away from the Nile, away from the land he had known all his life, walked over the crest of the hill and down into a valley.

Ramose couldn't imagine why the desert was called the Red Land, when it all seemed to be a dirty yellow colour. The slope below him was covered in sharp rocks and flints where a cliff had long ago collapsed. He could just make out a mud brick village on the valley floor the same colour as the desert hills around it. If he hadn't been looking for it, he might not have even seen the village. From a distance it could easily have been a natural feature, shaped by the winds. There was no green, no gold, no sign of life. This was his new home—the village of the tomb makers.

Over the next hill, he knew, was the Great Place, the valley that his father had chosen for his tomb and for the tombs of future pharaohs. It was a special place, a place sacred to the gods, where Pharaoh hoped his tomb would be safe from tomb robbers.

Ramose had refused to leave the city at first. As a prince he was used to getting his own way. But the more he'd thought about it, the more he knew Heria and Keneben were right. He wouldn't be safe in the palace. Queen Mutnofret was a strong-willed and powerful woman who was feared by servants and officials alike. Eventually Ramose had agreed to their plan. He would live secretly as an apprentice scribe until Keneben and Heria could find proof of Queen Mutnofret's treachery against him and his brothers. They would seek out the people who had provided the poison, the ones who had rigged his brother's chariot accident and buy the truth with gold. It would be no more than six months, they said.

Keneben had found a scribe called Paneb in the tomb makers' village who was looking for a boy to take on as an apprentice. The scribe had had a local boy in mind for the job, but a large sum in gold and copper had convinced him that Ramose would be a better choice.

Ramose rehearsed his new life story in his head as he walked. He had been born in a distant part of Egypt far to the south. He was the son of a local official and had been trained to follow in his father's footsteps. A terrible disease had swept the town though, and both his parents had died. He had miraculously survived and been brought up by an uncle in the city. The uncle had recently died too, leaving him with no one to care for him. Ramose hoped he'd got all the details right.

5

THE RED LAND

THE TOMB MAKERS' village didn't look very welcoming. A high mud brick wall surrounded it. There was just one entrance. Ramose was exhausted. The journey from the city had taken less than two hours, but the prince had never walked so far in his life. It was past noon and he was hungry and thirsty.

There was one street in the village and it was

empty. It hardly even deserved to be called a street. It was just the space between two rows of houses. Keneben's map showed the scribe's house about halfway along the street and on the left-hand side. There weren't that many houses, the whole village would have fitted into one corner of the palace.

Ramose was soon standing outside the house with Paneb's name inscribed above the door. Even though he was tired and hungry, he had a strong urge to turn and run all the way back to the palace and tell Keneben that he'd changed his mind. The door suddenly opened and a small figure burst out and nearly knocked him over. It was a young girl.

Ramose stared at her. He couldn't help it. Her skin was as dark as Nile mud. She had large rings in her ears and a string of fat orange beads around her neck. Her hair was a mass of tight black curls. She wore a length of coarse-looking material with broad stripes in green and red over her head. Around her waist was a strange belt made of intricately folded cloth. She glared back at Ramose.

"What are you staring at?"

No one had ever spoken to Ramose in that way before. He opened his mouth to call for the guards and have the girl taken away. He closed his mouth again, standing on the doorstep in confusion. The girl looked him up and down, at his broken sandals, dusty garment and sweating face.

"The boy's here," she called over her shoulder and then she ran off down the street.

A man appeared at the doorway.

"You're late," he said. "We were expecting you earlier."

Paneb wasn't at all like Ramose had imagined him. He'd had a vague picture in his head of a younger man who smiled a lot, someone like Keneben. The scribe was an old man, much older than Ramose's father, his hair was grey, his skin lined and he was fat. His stomach hung over his kilt and he had a number of chins.

"I was held up at the river," Ramose lied.

"You better come in."

Three steps led down from the street into the scribe's house. The house was so narrow, Ramose felt that if he stretched out his arms he could have touched both walls at once. The scribe led him into a room where two women were waiting. One was Ianna, the scribe's wife, the other was Teti, their servant.

"This is Ramose," Paneb told the women.

"The same name as the poor prince," said Ianna, who was fat like her husband.

Ramose nodded. Heria had wanted him to take another name, but he thought he might lose himself completely if he didn't at least have his real name.

"Such a sad thing for a boy to die so young," she said.

"Very unfortunate," said Paneb. "Such a rush to get his tomb ready."

The servant brought in a tray of food.

"We've already eaten our midday meal," said the scribe. "But you're probably hungry after your journey."

Ramose was hungry. He watched as the servant put bread and meat, cooked vegetables and fruit on a low table. It was a small amount of food that had obviously been picked over already and then left uncovered to dry out. Several flies circled the food. The meat was from a pig. Ramose had never eaten anything but the best quality beef. If he'd been at the palace he would have kicked over the table and demanded fresh food. He was very hungry though.

Ramose sat and waited for Teti to serve him and to pour something for him to drink. She didn't move. There was an awkward silence. Paneb and his wife watched him with puzzled expressions. "Is there something wrong?" asked Ianna.

"No," said Ramose.

He looked at the food. The others looked at him. Ramose suddenly realised that he had to serve himself. He moved over to the table and helped himself to the food. The bread was gritty and the meat was tough. All there was to drink was beer, which had a bitter taste.

"May I have some gazelle's milk?" he asked. He was pleased that he had remembered to ask politely instead of demanding it.

The servant looked surprised and shook her head. Paneb and his wife exchanged doubtful looks. Ramose ate his meal in silence.

When he had finished the meagre meal, the servant brought him a bowl of water to wash his hands. He had to be grateful for small blessings.

"Where is my room?" he asked the scribe.

"You don't have a room," Paneb replied. "You will sleep on the roof. My wife has a chest for you to keep your things in."

Ramose had never been in an ordinary house before. It was tiny, just three rooms and an outdoor kitchen. There was only one bedroom and that was where Paneb and his wife slept. The servant woman and the girl slept out in the garden.

Teti carried the chest up to the roof for Ramose. The chest wasn't made of wood but woven from date palm leaves. It was rather old and the leather hinges didn't look too strong. Ramose unpacked his few possessions and put them in the trunk. All that Heria and Keneben had allowed him to bring was a spare kilt, some scratchy undergarments and a woollen cloak. Keneben had given him some gold shaped into large ring-shaped ingots in case of emergencies. He hid them under everything else. He also put his scribe's kit in the chest. He realised that his own ebony brush box and palette, inlaid with ivory, gold and turquoise, would be too rich for a humble scribe. He would have to pretend he had lost his scribe's tools and ask Paneb to provide new ones.

Paneb, like the other workers, worked an eight-day shift at the pharaoh's tomb, followed by two days rest. This was his second rest day, he would be returning to work the next day. That gave Ramose the rest of the afternoon to explore the house and the village. Half an hour would have been enough really. It took ten minutes to walk the length of the one street. The fifteen or so houses were built squashed up against each other and all looked the same.

Outside the village walls there was a small temple, a half-finished building almost as large as the village and a lot of sand and rocks.

What was there to amuse a boy in this miserable place? There were no gardens, no ponds, no orchards, no river. No animals to hunt, no fish to catch. A group of boys about the same age as Ramose were playing a game that involved drawing lines in the sand. It looked very dull.

They all looked at him as he walked by, but no one spoke.

When he got back to the scribe's house, he wondered what he was going to do with himself for the rest of the day. Wandering around, he found the dark-skinned girl out in the garden. She was on her hands and knees grinding grain on a curved stone.

"So you're the new apprentice," she said.

"And who are you?" Ramose demanded.

"My name is Karoya," she said, "I grind the grain." She sprinkled more wheat grains on the curved surface and rolled a round stone back and forth over them.

"You're a slave, aren't you," said Ramose. "Are you from Kush?"

"Yes. Not that it's any business of yours."

"I don't think you should talk to me like that," said Ramose.

"Why not?"

Ramose didn't know what to say to this insolent girl.

"Where I come from you'd be beaten for such rudeness."

"And who's going to beat me?" laughed Karoya. "Certainly not a puny little apprentice scribe, like you. You'd have to catch me first."

"Where are the rest of the servants?" asked Ramose changing the subject.

"There aren't any more servants, just Teti and me."

"But who will dress me? Who will help me bathe?"

"Who will dress you?" Karoya stopped grinding and looked up at him in amazement. "Only babies can't dress themselves."

Ramose looked at the shocked expression on the girl's face and realised he'd made another mistake.

"I was just joking," he said, and went back into the house. Ramose didn't like making mistakes. He didn't like having to pretend he was an ordinary person. There was nothing about his new life that he liked.

Ramose had been looking forward to washing off the dust and sweat from his walk. Water was precious out there in the desert. He was only allowed to have two jars of water to bathe with. It was such a small amount of water. He was also given a tiny jar of animal fat mixed with limestone to cleanse his skin. He knocked over one of the jars, spilling most of the water meant for rinsing, leaving his skin covered with the chalky fat. So much for bathing, thought Ramose. I probably smell worse now than I did before.

That night Ramose lay on his back. Then he lay on his left side. Next he tried his right side. It didn't matter which way he lay he just couldn't get comfortable. How could he? How could anybody be expected to sleep lying out on the roof on a rickety old bed with a base of woven reeds? He'd only been given one thin blanket. Nights in the desert were cold. Even wrapped in his cloak he was freezing.

Ramose was still awake when the sun rose. His body, used to soft beds, was sore from head to toe. He was itchy as well. When he inspected his legs and arms, he saw that they were covered in bites. Whether they were from the mosquitoes that had buzzed around his head all night or from the fleas he had found in the blanket, he wasn't sure.

He put on his kilt. He fumbled with the ties. When he had finished it hung unevenly. He wrapped it the other way and it hung a little better, though he was sure he wouldn't be able to undo the knot he'd tied.

Breakfast was the same gritty bread and a few overripe figs.

"I'd prefer some sweet plum cake," he said to Teti.

She blinked at him as if he'd asked for a slice of the moon.

Scribe Paneb and his wife came in for their breakfast. They grabbed at the food with both hands, filling their mouths. Ianna talked and ate at the same time. Ramose suddenly lost his appetite. He went back up to the roof, where he found the slave girl just lifting the lid of his chest.

"Take your hands off my belongings!" shouted Ramose.

"I was just going to tidy them for you," said the girl.

"Your job is to grind grain and make bread, not to touch my personal things. You were looking for something to steal, I know. My father told me that people from Kush were all thieves and barbarians!"

"I wasn't stealing anything," retorted Karoya. "Why would I want to steal your spare kilt and your undergarments?"

Ramose marched down the stairs. The scribe was still eating his breakfast.

"I found the slave girl up on the roof trying to steal my possessions," Ramose said to Paneb. "I want her punished."

"I've told her before about being inquisitive," said the scribe belching softly.

"Inquisitive!" shouted Ramose. "She's a thief. She should be beaten."

"I don't think that will be necessary," said Ianna. "She can't work as hard if she's bruised and sore."

"She can go without her evening meal," said the scribe.

Ramose couldn't understand why the scribe was being so lenient with the girl.

"It's hard to punish someone who has nothing," observed the scribe.

Ramose turned on his heel and went back up the stairs two at a time.

"That's it," he said to himself as he rammed his belongings back into the reed bag. "I'm leaving!'

6

PHARAOH'S TOMB

RAMOSE HAD had enough. He couldn't stay in that place with those people. He just couldn't. He strode down the village street. How could he be expected to live in such a squalid little house with such disrespectful people? He'd rather eat the palace scraps than their awful food. He'd have to explain to Heria and Keneben. It just wasn't right for a prince to have to sleep on a flea-ridden bed out in the open and to have to put up with barbarians trying to steal what few possessions he had. It was too much.

Ramose slung his bag on his shoulder and walked out of the village gate. Worrying about being stabbed or poisoned would be much easier than living in that horrible place. He missed his sister, he missed Keneben and Heria, he missed the river, he missed being waited on. He got ten strides away from the village when a voice called out.

"Where do you think you're going?"

Ramose turned round. It was the slave girl, Karoya. She was sitting in the shade under the wall of the half-built mud brick building outside the village.

"I'm going home," Ramose replied continuing to stride away from the village. "Away from thieves and fat scribes."

"I thought you were an orphan and you didn't have a home."

"I mean the city," said Ramose still walking.

"Why would you want to go to that noisy, smelly place?"

"The part I lived in wasn't noisy and smelly."

"I thought your uncle died and you had no one to care for you."

Ramose stopped walking. He imagined returning to the palace. The only people he could really depend upon were his sister and two servants. The queen and the vizier wanted him dead. Everyone believed he was dead already. He might not survive there for half an hour. He sat down in the sand.

"I hate the desert."

"I love the desert," said Karoya.

"There's nothing in the desert to love. Nothing but sand and rocks."

"It's beautiful. It reminds me of my home. I come out here every morning to watch the sunrise. The sky turns pink and orange and purple."

Ramose looked up at the early morning sky. The colours were beautiful, like a temple painting. Voices were drifting from the village. The first tomb workers were dawdling out of the gate, talking quietly to themselves as they headed off to work.

"I want to go home," said Ramose sadly.

"This is your home now. You just have to get used to it."

"Don't tell me what I have to do! You have no idea what I've been through."

"I know what it's like to have to leave your home and live in a foreign place full of strangers," said the girl.

Ramose sighed and leaned against the wall. "What's this building for?" he asked.

"It's a house for Pharaoh," said Karoya.

"A palace?" Ramose looked at the rough half-finished walls. "This is nothing like a palace."

"It's supposed to be for the pharaoh if he ever comes to visit. The men work on it from time to time."

"Why would Pharaoh ever want to come to this awful place?"

Karoya shrugged. "So are you leaving?"

"No."

It was now fully light.

"The scribe will be looking for you," said Karoya. "Go and wait for him at the gate. He'll think you were keen to get started."

"I don't know why you think I should take the advice of a thief," Ramose grumbled bitterly.

"I'm not a thief," said Karoya.

Ramose went over to the gate to wait for the scribe.

Paneb walked in silence. Ramose was grateful. He didn't want to talk to the scribe. He followed Paneb up the hill to the west of the village, further into the desert, further away from his home. The overweight scribe was soon puffing and panting. The other workers disappeared over the crest before Paneb and Ramose were halfway up.

The path looked the same as the one that had brought him to the village—just a dusty track worn by the passage of feet. On either side of the path was the same dry sand and sharp rocks and

flints. There were no trees, no plants, no sign of
animal life. Ramose thought it must surely be
the most inhospitable place in the world. They
reached the top and the heat of the sun hit
Ramose full in the face. He wasn't used to being
outside in the heat without servants to fan him.
He hoped he would be able to work out in the sun
without fainting.

Ramose shielded his eyes. The Great Place lay
below them. It didn't look great at all. It was a
dry and sand-coloured valley the same as the
valley where the village was. The only difference
was the cliffs leading down to this valley floor
were still standing.

"Is this it?" asked Ramose. "Where's Pharaoh's
tomb?"

"Hidden underground, of course," said Paneb.
"The entrance is over there."

He pointed to a hole in the side of the valley
wall opposite. Ramose was disappointed. He
knew that the royal tomb was being built
underground to protect it from tomb robbers, but
he had expected it to have an ornate entrance
and elaborate temples above ground. There was
nothing.

The path wove up and down until it found a
way down around the cliffs. When they reached
the valley floor, Ramose could see the entrance
more clearly. It was just a large square hole cut

into the rock face. Outside were blocks of stone quarried from the tomb. The tomb makers were nowhere to be seen. Paneb muttered grumpily to himself as he headed to the tomb entrance. An enormous man stood at the entrance. He wasn't an Egyptian, he was black-skinned, like Karoya, and very tall.

"Good morning, Scribe Paneb," said the guard.

"Morning," grumbled Paneb.

"Who is this with you?" asked the guard.

"This is my new apprentice, Ramose. Let him pass whenever he wishes."

Paneb also introduced Ramose to Samut, a sweaty man with long stringy hair who was foreman of the tomb workers. Then they were out of the sun and suddenly in darkness. They walked down a steeply sloping corridor that led deep inside the rock. Small oil lamps lit the way at intervals, but it was still very dark. Ramose was surprised. He wasn't really sure what a scribe attached to a royal tomb was meant to do, but he'd imagined that he would be working out in the blazing sun. It had never occurred to him that he would be working deep underground.

They passed a group of sculptors working on carvings on the sloping walls of the corridor. Ramose could make out pictures of his father fighting in military campaigns. There was a carving of him firing arrows from a chariot, a

carving of him with his foot on the head of a
grovelling barbarian, another of him standing
next to a pile of dismembered hands, cut from his
victims. Hieroglyphs told the story of his bravery
and how he was undefeated in battle. The corridor
continued to slope steeply down. Ramose looked
over his shoulder. The tomb entrance was just a
small square of light high above him.

The corridor opened into a room where men
were working on the ceiling. It was painted
deep blue and the painters, clinging to a wooden
scaffold, were covering it with five-pointed yellow
stars. The murmur of voices and the sound of
the chipping of stone drifted up from a flight
of steps that led down from this room at right
angles. Ramose followed Paneb down the steps.
The burial chamber was at the bottom. Outliners
were marking out paintings and text on four
square columns supporting the ceiling. More
sculptors were on their hands and knees carving
a large red sandstone sarcophagus.

Ramose wasn't interested in the detail of the
carving though. As soon as he'd lost sight of the
square of light that was the outside, he felt panic
rise in him. He was thinking about how far it was
to the surface. He was picturing the enormous
weight of rock just above his head and imagining
it falling in and burying him alive. His breathing
started to get fast and shallow. The air was stale

and smelt of rock dust, burning oil and sweat. His skin turned icy cold. The walls were closing in on him. He was sure he was about to be crushed to death. He choked out some words.

"Outside," he stammered. "Can't breathe."

He stumbled towards the stairs, falling over a sculptor.

"Where do you think you're going?" the scribe asked impatiently. The tomb workers were all laughing.

He felt his way up the stairs. His chest felt like it was exploding. He couldn't draw a breath. He scrambled under the scaffolding, tripped over a jar of paint and crawled along the floor. A square of daylight came into view. Ramose rested his cheek on the cold stone floor and breathed in the fresh air that came from above.

"Whoever heard of a tomb worker afraid of being underground?" said one of the tomb workers. They all thought it was a great joke.

"You'll have to get used to being underground," Paneb snapped. "I can't have the workers laughing at me. You get used to it or you go."

"I'll be all right," Ramose said in a quiet, croaky voice.

"Whether you're all right or not, you have work to do," said Paneb angrily. "You must keep a tally of the copper chisels that the sculptors use."

The scribe sat down on a block of stone.

"Whenever a chisel wears out it is to be replaced. Go back up, out to the valley and collect some new chisels from the store. There are men up there in the corridor with worn out chisels, we can't have them sitting around doing nothing."

The scribe was, however, quite happy to sit and do nothing himself.

"Where is the papyrus I am to write on?" Ramose asked.

Paneb looked around quickly, hoping that the workers hadn't heard.

"Where did you get this apprentice from, Paneb?" shouted one. "Are you sure he knows how to write?" The painters were all chuckling to themselves.

"We don't use papyrus in the tomb," hissed Paneb. "Whatever gave you that idea? It's very expensive as I'm sure you know."

"So what do I write on?"

The scribe sighed at the ignorance of his apprentice. "On stone flakes, of course. The pieces chipped from the rock when the quarry men were excavating the tomb. You'll find plenty of them in piles up on the surface, all different sizes. I use papyrus only for the documents I send to Vizier Wersu."

Ramose shivered. Whether it was the mention of the vizier's name or the cool air in the tomb he wasn't sure. Either way he was glad to be making his way out of the tomb and up into fresh air again, even if it was hot desert air.

Out on the valley floor Ramose stood in the sun and felt it heat up his skin. He looked up at the clear blue sky and the bright sun until his breathing slowed and he felt calm again. Ramose looked around the valley, now dotted with after-images of the sun. The scribe was right, there were piles of stone flakes outside the tomb entrance: small ones no bigger than a hand which could be used for short notes, larger ones for long reports.

The mud brick storehouse was about fifty paces from the tomb entrance. Another huge, dark-skinned foreigner stood on guard outside. Ramose explained who he was and the guard let him enter. The storeroom was packed with everything that the tomb makers needed: paints, tools, oil for the lamps as well as grain and water.

"Treat these very carefully," said the storekeeper taking a dozen copper chisels from a wooden chest. "The workers like their chisels sharp, and Scribe Paneb gets very angry if anybody damages them." He wrapped them carefully in a strip of linen. "One of these chisels is worth about six of those bags of wheat." He jerked his head in the direction of the food stores. "That's three months wages for you."

A boy was stacking sacks of grain. He was one

of the boys whom Ramose had seen playing a game outside the village.

Ramose took the chisels from the storeman. He walked out into the hot air again, pushing the chisels into the belt of his kilt. The other boy hurried out of the storehouse behind Ramose and knocked his elbow so that the chisels fell out of his grasp and onto the rocky ground. He didn't stop to apologise. He kept walking, turning for just long enough to give Ramose a glare full of hatred.

Ramose called out to the storeman. "Did you see that? Did you see what he did?"

7

A LETTER
FROM HOME

THE STOREMAN shrugged and went back to his work. Ramose was furious. He took out his anger on a nearby rock. All that achieved was a bleeding toe. He collected up the scattered chisels. Three of them were damaged. He knew he'd get the blame for this.

Paneb was very angry about the damaged chisels. Ramose showed him the stone flake on which he'd recorded the workers who had received new chisels. Paneb wasn't very happy about that either.

"Is that the best writing you can do?" he said incredulously. "I can only read half of it." He turned the stone flake around, making a big show of how difficult it was to read. "You'll have to rewrite it. In fact you can rewrite the whole thing ten times to make sure you get it right."

Ramose didn't complain. He was glad to have an excuse to get out of the tomb. He found a tiny wedge of shade outside the tomb entrance and sat down to rewrite the details about the chisels. He remembered the stories that Keneben had made him write out about how wonderful it was to be a scribe.

"Ramose!" Paneb's voice echoed up the tomb shaft. "Come here, boy."

So far Ramose couldn't think of anything good about being a scribe. You might get to sit down a lot of the time and you didn't have to lift blocks of stone the size of small houses, but it wasn't much fun. He trudged back down into the darkness of the tomb past the sculptors, his heart already starting to race at the thought of being shut off from the light. Fortunately, Paneb only wanted a cup of water and Ramose was soon climbing back up the sloping corridor again. The back of his legs ached already.

By midday Ramose had walked up and down the tomb shaft at least ten times. It seemed that every time he got to the bottom of the shaft, Paneb remembered something he wanted from above. Every time he found a patch of shade to sit down in above ground, Paneb's voice would echo up the shaft and he was needed down below.

The other workers gathered in groups to eat their midday meal. Ramose ate his gritty bread, dried fish and figs by himself. The other apprentices sat in a group of their own. He caught them looking at him a couple of times, but none of them came over to talk to him.

By the end of the day Ramose's legs ached so much and he was so tired that he just wanted to go to sleep.

"Where do we sleep?" Ramose asked Paneb when the scribe came panting up the shaft.

Paneb pointed to some piles of rocks on the valley floor opposite the storehouse. Ramose looked closer. He'd thought that they were more discarded rocks. Now he could see that they were actually low huts made from the sharp rocks that lay around on the valley floor stacked up on top of each other. The huts were roofed over with dead palm branches that must have been carried all the way up from the river.

"You can sleep with the other apprentices," Paneb said. "I can't have you in my hut. I don't sleep well and the sound of unfamiliar breathing would keep me awake."

The three boys were sitting outside their hut.

"Scribe Paneb said I should share your hut," Ramose told them.

No one replied. Ramose went inside. The flea-ridden bed back at the scribe's house now seemed like the height of comfort. His chamber in the palace with the painted walls and the bed with the soft mattress was a dim memory. All he had to sleep on was a reed mat spread on the bare ground. He was too tired to eat. He just wanted to close his eyes. He got out his cloak and wrapped himself up in it, even though the sun had barely set.

The other boys had different ideas though. After they had eaten, they came inside the hut and played board games. Ramose had played similar games back at the palace with Keneben. It had always been a quiet business. The games the boys played involved a lot of shouting and disputing. One of the boys was a bad loser. He always accused the others of cheating, but he would do anything to win himself. Whenever Ramose was about to drift off to sleep, one of the boys would shout out or nudge him with a foot. When they were ready to sleep, they each took it in turns to keep Ramose awake while the others slept. Ramose hardly slept at all.

In the morning Ramose stood in line to receive his breakfast. His stomach growled with hunger. He took his bread and dried fruit and was pleased to see that there was milk to drink. Just as he went to sit down with his food, one of the boys pushed him from behind and the food, milk and Ramose himself ended up in the sand. The tomb workers all laughed.

"That apprentice of yours has got two left feet, Paneb."

Ramose hated them all. He wanted to make them all suffer the same as he was, but he knew anything he said or did would only make them laugh at him more. He swallowed his anger and picked up the remains of his meal.

The job of an apprentice scribe was to keep a register of all the workers reporting for work every morning. If someone was late, he recorded it. If someone didn't come, he had to find out if they had a good excuse, such as being sick or having a special family feast day. He recorded that too. Then he had to note down all the tools they took from the store, all the pigment used to make paint, all the oil and wicks for the lamps. Even the water was rationed. The nearest water was the Nile and it had to be carried up by donkey from the river in big jars. Each man was only allowed six cups a day to drink.

Ramose collected the worn and broken chisels and took them back to the storeman. Copper was expensive and the chisels would be melted down and made into new chisels. At least once a day, Ramose dropped one of the stone flakes that he was writing on and had to pick up the pieces and fit them together again before he could copy the writing onto a fresh flake. He also had to walk up and down the steep stone ramp to the tomb again and again. Sometimes it was to fetch things from the store; sometimes it was to fetch a cup of water for Paneb. Paneb didn't do much at all.

The pace of work at the tomb was leisurely. Pharaoh was in good health and expected to live for another five or ten years at least. No one was in a great hurry to finish the work.

At meal times and in the evenings, the three boys did their best to make Ramose's life a misery. They never spoke to him, but from what they said to each other he got to know each of them. Nakhtamun was a short, stocky boy with a squashed nose and a shaved head. He was an apprentice sculptor. Hapu was an apprentice painter. He was quieter than the other two and always had a worried look as if he was sure he was going to get into trouble at any minute. Weni was the ringleader of the little group.

Weni was angry. It was he who had made Ramose drop the chisels. He was the boy who was going to be apprentice scribe before Ramose came along. Now he was just a general errand boy at the tomb. Eventually he would have to leave and join the army or work in the fields. He was a sullen boy with a down-turned mouth, hard eyes and a scar on his cheek from a fight he once had with a sculptor wielding a chisel. Weni never smiled. Even when he won at senet he just scowled triumphantly at his opponents. The other two boys did whatever Weni said. The three boys hated Ramose. They wanted to get rid of him so that Weni could take his place.

Ramose tried to tell Samut, the foreman, about his problems with the boys, but the man wasn't interested.

"Sort out your own problems," he said. "Don't come telling tales to me."

This seemed most unjust to Ramose until he later found out that the foreman was Weni's uncle.

At the end of the eight-day shift, Ramose left the Great Place with relief. He didn't know if he had the strength to go back there again. The scribe's house now seemed large and bright. He collapsed onto the rickety bed which seemed unbelievably comfortable. His legs ached so much, he thought he might never get up again.

The next day, Ramose felt better after his first

full night's sleep in eight days. He had something important to do. After breakfast, he told the scribe he was going out for a walk.

"You're not going to try to run away again are you?" asked Karoya who was out in the garden grinding grain as usual.

"I don't have to tell you what I'm doing," snapped Ramose.

He walked briskly up the path that led towards the city, despite his sore legs. He wasn't running away though.

At the top of the hill he left the path and took ten measured paces to the north and then five to the east. There was a rock formation that looked a little like a lion ready to pounce. Ramose walked around it.

At the base, just where the lion's back paw would have been, there was a hollow. Ramose reached inside the hollow. Something was in there. He pulled out a small papyrus scroll. Ramose held the papyrus to his chest and smiled. It was a letter from Keneben. The tutor had arranged to leave a note for him after every shift at the tomb. Ramose broke open the seal and read the note eagerly.

The tutor Keneben greets his young lord, in life, prosperity and health and in the favour of Amun, King of the Gods, as well as Thoth, Lord of

God's words. May they give you favour, love and
cleverness whatever you do. How are you,
my lord? I am well as is your nanny, Heria. We
are both well. Tomorrow is in Ra's hands. We
work at our common goal and matters go well.
Your royal sister, Hatshepsut, has good health.
Write a note to us so that our hearts may be
happy.

The note told Ramose nothing really, but it made him feel like singing. He read the letter again and again, running his hands over the rough surface of the papyrus and smelling its musky fragrance. He pictured Keneben in the palace schoolroom teaching Hatshepsut.

He then pulled out a stone flake from his bag. He took out his palette and reed pens, as well as a small jar of water. He sat cross-legged with his back against the lion rock, dipped a pen in the water, rubbed it on the ink block and wrote a note back to his friends.

He thought of complaining about the miserable life he had, the awful food, the rickety bed and how everyone treated him badly. In the end though, he didn't complain. He didn't want Heria worrying about him. Instead he wrote that he had seen his father's tomb, that he missed them both and that he was counting the days until he could see their faces again.

He let the ink dry in the sun and then he put the stone flake into the hollow for Keneben to collect.

Once or twice he thought he heard noises and wondered if someone had followed him, but it was just the sounds of rocks cracking in the heat or shifting with the wind. He looked towards the Nile and imagined he could smell the fertile smells of the river valley and see the white walls of the palace. Then he turned and went back to the village.

8

A LAPIS LAZULI HEART

THE NEXT SHIFT was not much different to the previous one, with one exception—this time Weni spoke to him.

Weni was unpacking food that had been sent up from the city on donkeys. Ramose was sitting out in his wedge of shade just outside the tomb entrance. He was transferring all his notes about the tomb workers' attendance from a dozen small stone chips onto one large stone flake the size of a serving platter. He carefully copied down his notes for each day and totalled them up. Paneb would then recopy the details onto a papyrus scroll to be sent to the vizier at the end of the month.

Ramose sat back and looked at his work. Keneben would have been proud of him. His writing was in almost straight lines, apart from where the irregular stone surface went up and down. He smiled to himself and put it on the ground to dry in the sun. That's when Weni came up to him.

"Why don't you just go back where you came from?" Weni spat the words with hatred. "No one wants you here."

"I wouldn't be here if I didn't have to be," Ramose replied.

Weni was on his way down into the tomb with a water jar for the workers.

"You take this down, I don't feel like doing it," Weni said holding out the clay jar. The scar on his face and his small, hard eyes gave him a cruel look.

"Take it yourself," said Ramose.

A malicious look flashed into Weni's eyes. He tipped the jar sideways and water spilled all over Ramose's stone flake. His carefully written words quickly dissolved into grey swirls in the water, and washed off the stone. Ramose watched as his work soaked into the sand.

"Look what you've done!" he shouted. "That took me nearly half a day."

"Serves you right," replied Weni. His mouth was twisted unpleasantly. It was the closest Ramose had seen him get to smiling. "You should have done as you were told."

Ramose stared at the blank stone flake. All his hard work was washed away. A few weeks ago that would have made him fly into a rage. Since he'd been in the Great Place his anger had been replaced by despair. He was powerless and alone there. Anger was pointless.

Ramose had to write his notes again after the workday was finished. Weni and the other boys wouldn't let him work in the hut. They suddenly needed an early night and complained when he lit a lamp. He went outside, looking for a place where his light wouldn't be seen. Inside the mouth of the tomb was the perfect spot. Ramose asked the night guard and he didn't seem to mind. It took him several hours.

When he had finished, Ramose didn't want to risk leaving it in his own hut in case one of the other boys got hold of it. Instead he carried it carefully to the scribe's hut. It was a moonless night and Ramose was scared he would trip and drop the stone flake and ruin his work again.

He entered Paneb's hut, ready to apologise for waking the scribe, but he was snoring deeply and didn't hear him. Ramose was tired but somehow not sleepy. He sat outside and looked up at the stars. He preferred the desert at night.

Ramose went to see Paneb before breakfast. He thought the scribe might be pleased with his work. He wasn't. Instead he grumbled about the lamp oil Ramose had used during the night.

"It has been reported to the foreman," complained Paneb. "You'll have to pay for the extra oil out of your wages."

Ramose sighed. It was stupid of him to think he could please the scribe. Paneb would never be happy. What did it matter? Ramose reminded himself that he was Pharaoh's son. One day he would be pharaoh. One day the workers who laughed at him, the boys who made his life so miserable, the grumpy scribe, they would all be working on his tomb. He would personally inspect their work. He would instruct them to make sculptures of the time he went into hiding in the Great Place. The pictures would tell the story of how he worked like a common man in order to foil the plans of his enemies at the palace. The tomb makers would remember how they had treated him and would beg their pharaoh's forgiveness. Ramose was looking forward to that day.

In the meantime, he had one more day in his current shift. He couldn't wait for the two days rest. Most of all he was looking forward to getting another letter from Keneben. He knew that if he could survive two shifts at the Great Place he could survive eighteen. That would be the end of the six months. Then his tutor and dear Heria would have prepared everything for his return to the palace. He found a small stone flake and made eighteen marks on it. He crossed one off. At the end of the day he would be able to cross off another.

That evening as he walked back to the tomb makers' village, Ramose felt good for the first time in a long while—since before Topi died. Nothing could spoil his good mood, not Paneb's grumbling, Weni's snide remarks or the sculptors' taunts.

When he got to the scribe's house, he greeted Ianna cheerfully and ran up the stairs to the roof so that he could get his clean kilt. When he got to the top of the stairs he stopped dead. Karoya was sitting on his bed with her arms folded. Spread out on the bed beside her were the contents of his chest.

"I told you not to touch my things," said Ramose angrily. "If you've stolen anything—"

"Who are you?" Karoya asked calmly.

"You know who I am."

"I know that you have a fine set of scribe's tools inlaid with ivory and jewels, yet you use the plain, old worn tools given to you by scribe Paneb." She picked up the gold rings. "And this gold must be worth a year's food rations for a whole family."

"I don't have to explain my possessions to a barbarian slave!" Ramose was trying to sound calm, but he wasn't.

"I've always felt there was something curious about you. When you first came, you hardly even knew how to tie your own kilt. And no orphan boy is used to drinking gazelle's milk. I want to know who you are."

Ramose snatched back the gold rings and wrapped them up again.

"And there's another thing about you," said the girl.

"What?"

"You are very rude. Egyptians are strange people, but they are polite. They always say thank you, even to a slave girl. You never do."

"If you tell anyone about this, I'll…" He could not think of anything to do to Karoya.

He needed time to think. He ran out of the house, out of the village and didn't stop till he got to the lion rock, his chest heaving, his breath rasping. He thrust his hand into the hollow. He had an awful feeling there would be no message for him, but his groping hand found not only a roll

of parchment, but also a knotted linen parcel. He
pulled them out with relief, broke the seal on the
papyrus and read the message.

*My prince, my heart is in mourning, I am
crouched with my head on my knees. The news
I have will bring you nothing but grief. Heria,
your beloved nanny, is resting from life.
She did not suffer but died peacefully in her
sleep. There is other news, less sorrowful but
still unwelcome. The queen has been in your
father's ear. She has appointed a new tutor for
her son, Prince Tuthmosis. I have been posted
abroad to the land of Punt. I have said farewell
to the Princess Hatshepsut. By the time you read
this letter, I will have left. Your secret is safe still.
I do not know when I will be able to contact you
again. My prayers will be with you every day.*

Ramose's shaking hands untied the linen bundle.
Inside was a beautiful blue jewel, almost too big
to fit into his hand. It was made from lapis lazuli
and shaped like a large beetle. It was edged in
gold and had two red garnets set in the stone
for eyes. On the beetle's back were carved the
three hieroglyphs that made up Ramose's name.
He turned over the jewel. The flat bottom was
covered with more hieroglyphs, tiny and finely
carved. It was his heart scarab, made to be buried

with his mummified body, wrapped tightly next to his heart. There was another scribbled note with it. It told briefly how Heria had managed to take this heart scarab from the dead body of the village boy. She had replaced the scarab with a ceramic one with the boy's own name on it. Hopefully the priests would not notice. Ramose looked at the scarab. It was so bright and so beautiful out there in the bleak, colourless desert.

Ramose sank down on his knees in the sand. In the last weeks he had held back his sadness, he had buried his loneliness, he had hidden his fears. Now he couldn't hold it in any longer. He had believed that his two friends would save him, now they were both gone. Heria, the nanny who had cared for him all his life, was lost to him forever. Keneben, his tutor, was far away in a foreign land. His father believed he was dead, and so did his beloved sister. The queen who hated him was still in the palace, still the pharaoh's favourite. He was alone in the world. Tears dropped one by one into the sand and disappeared, sucked into its dryness. Ramose wept and wept until the sand beneath his face was wet.

A hand touched his shoulder. Ramose looked up, startled. His first thought was that the palace guards had been sent to get him. It was Karoya.

"What's wrong, Ramose?" she asked.

Ramose wiped his face on his kilt.

"Why does the writing sadden you so?"

Karoya stroked his arm gently, just like Heria used to do when he was upset. She looked at him with what seemed like real concern. Then she suddenly stopped stroking. She was staring at the scarab in Ramose's hand.

"Where did you get that? I've never seen such a jewel."

Ramose sat back with the scarab in his lap, but said nothing.

"What sort of an apprentice scribe has such a thing and two handfuls of gold and scribe's equipment fit for a king?"

Ramose said nothing.

"Who are you?" asked Karoya peering at Ramose.

"You ask a lot of questions," he said.

Ramose felt that he had nothing more to lose. He needed to know that there was at least one person in Egypt who knew who he was and why he was in hiding.

"I am Prince Ramose," he said, trying his best to sound royal even though his face was streaked with dirt and tears. "Third son of the pharaoh. Heir to the throne of Egypt."

"The prince is dead. Even I know that."

"He's not dead. I'm not dead."

Karoya looked at the scarab, then at Ramose.

"Do you believe me?"

"That would explain a lot of your strangeness. Why would a prince be hiding in the village?"

Ramose told her the whole story, all about the deaths of his brothers, the evil queen, and his friends' fears for his life.

"My friends were supposed to be collecting evidence against the queen and the vizier, to convince the pharaoh that they had murdered my brothers and tried to murder me. Now my friends are gone there is no one in the world I can trust, apart from my sister, Hatshepsut, and she thinks I'm dead."

"You can trust me," said the slave girl. "I won't tell anybody."

Ramose looked at her and believed her.

"Thank you."

9

CARVED
IN STONE

KAROYA HAD kept her word and told no one what she had learned about Ramose. "Why do you have a jewel that is shaped like a beetle?" she asked as she kneaded bread dough in a large clay bowl.

"It's a heart scarab," replied Ramose who was sitting in the kitchen garden watching her.

"What's it for?"

"It's made to be buried with me when I die."

"It's very beautiful. It seems a shame to bury it in a tomb."

"When an Egyptian dies, their body is preserved so that it can travel into the afterlife."

Karoya glanced at him dubiously and started to shape the dough into flat round loaves.

"I've heard about this. They take out all the insides and wrap the body in strips of cloth."

"Not all of the insides—the heart is left in. In the afterlife Osiris, the god of the underworld, judges whether the person is fit to enter. Anubis, the jackal-headed god, takes the heart and weighs it against the feather of truth. If the heart exactly balances the weight of the feather, then Anubis knows the owner of the heart has been a good and truthful person and allows him to enter the afterlife."

Karoya fanned the small fire under the conical oven and added dry reeds and pats of animal dung to the flames.

"What happens if it doesn't balance?"

"Then the person is not fit for the afterlife. There is a monster called Ammut with the head of a crocodile, the front legs of a lion and the rear of a hippopotamus."

Karoya stopped fanning the fire.

"The monster comes and eats the heart of the bad person."

"And the beetle-shaped jewel?"

"It has my name on it. So that Osiris knows it is truly my heart. On the bottom of the scarab there is a prayer that no one will speak against me on that day of judgment."

Karoya took the rounds of dough and stuck them on the outside of the conical oven.

"Have you been a good person?" She didn't look him in the eyes as she usually did when she spoke to him.

Ramose had never really considered whether he was a good person or not. Would Osiris really question the goodness of Pharaoh's son?

"I'm not dead yet. When I am older, I will be pharaoh and I'll be a good pharaoh like my father. I'll treat my people well."

"And kill and enslave all foreigners," added Karoya.

The air was fragrant with the smell of baking bread.

"Maybe not."

The first loaf, now cooked, dropped to the ground.

"What are you going to do now?" Karoya asked quietly.

It was something Ramose had tried to avoid thinking about. The truth was he had no idea what to do.

"You only have two choices, as I see it," said

Karoya picking up the hot bread with the tips of her fingers. "You stay here and work in the Great Place or you go back to the city and let your father and sister know you are alive."

Ramose watched the other loaves fall from the oven one by one as they cooked. The thought of seeing his sister again lifted his heart.

"I have to go to the palace," he said after a while. "There's nothing else I can do." It felt good to make a decision. "I'll stay here until my father returns from his campaign."

Karoya picked up the other loaves and wrapped them in a cloth.

Ramose had begun to think that there was nothing he could do but stay forever in the Great Place counting chisels and recording absent workers. He'd imagined himself eating gritty bread and hearing people laughing at his clumsiness and making jokes about his fear of enclosed places till he was old and fat like Paneb. Talking to Karoya had helped him work out what he had to do. All he needed now was a plan, a way to get back into the palace.

In the meantime he would stay where he was and wait till his father returned from Kush. He had to work another shift at the Great Place.

Ramose decided to keep away from the other boys as much as he could. He would concentrate on the work he had to do and try and stay out of trouble. He found a quiet spot behind the storehouse and started working on a stone flake. He was writing out a list of the provisions that had arrived from the city: sacks of grain, piles of smelly fish, several oxen ready to be slaughtered and fresh vegetables too. All of this had to be allocated to the workers according to their roles in the tombs.

They were paid once a month. The scribe and the foreman earned the most, seven or eight sacks of grain, then came the sculptors and painters, who earned six sacks. The labourers who hauled blocks of stone and baskets of stone chips each got four and a half sacks. Finally came the apprentices who earned two sacks of grain each. The perishable food was divided up more or less equally among the workers. Ramose wrote down his own earnings: two sacks of grain, a dozen fish, one and a half deben of oxen meat, a jar of oil and a basket of vegetables.

Ramose wouldn't be seeing any of his earnings though. He had to pay for the three copper chisels he'd damaged and the oil he'd wasted staying up half the night rewriting. He also had to repay Paneb for his scribe's tools and for feeding him while he had no income. It would be several months before he would actually get any payment himself.

Ramose's concentration was broken. He could feel someone watching him. He looked up. It was Karoya.

"What are you doing up here?" he said. "Why aren't you back in the village?"

"I have to fillet and salt the fish," she said. "It has to be dried before it can be given out to the workers."

"So will you be staying here in the Great Place?"

"For a few days. I go where I am told."

"It will be a change to have a friend here," Ramose said. "Ever since I arrived, all I've done is make enemies."

Samut came over. "Get back to your work, slave girl," he shouted at Karoya and raised his hand to hit her.

"I told her to come over here," said Ramose. "I need to record how many fish she has gutted."

Samut walked away grumbling. Karoya smiled at Ramose and went back to her work.

Now that he was used to the work and the walking up and down the tomb ramp every day, Ramose wasn't ready to fall into bed as soon as his day's work was over. He was bored. In the evenings, the workers sat around in small groups talking. Some worked on private sculptures either for their own tombs or to sell to others. They made small statues of the gods or stelae, inscribed stones telling the gods all about the good things they had done in life. The painters sometimes brought up stools or small chests that they had made in the village. They painted them in their spare time and would sell them when they got home. The other boys often spent the evening playing games, but lately Weni had been working on a chest.

Ramose came back from the tomb carrying some stone flakes he wanted to check over before the sun set. Weni was sitting outside the hut carefully painting texts on the side of his chest in neat hieroglyphs. Ramose wasn't looking where he was going. He stumbled on a rock, staggered sideways to stop himself from falling over, and stood on Weni's chest. It was made of soft tamarisk wood, not hard imported wood. The chest splintered to pieces.

Weni was furious. His face turned red and he shouted angrily at Ramose, calling him every name he could think of.

"I'm sorry, Weni," said Ramose. "I didn't mean it. Truly."

"What difference does it make whether you meant it or not?" shouted Weni. "It's ruined anyway. Do you think I care whether you're sorry or not?"

After that incident Ramose decided to keep away from the hut until it got dark. He went for a long walk. He climbed the hills behind the Great Place. Not that there was anything to see. In those bare hills the most exciting thing that Ramose came across was a tuft of dry grass or a lizard slithering under a rock or a scorpion boldly warming itself in the lowering rays of the sun. Walking gave him time to think.

Ramose knew that when he went back to the palace, his problems wouldn't all be over. His father would welcome and protect him, he could be sure of that. His sister would rejoice that he was still alive, he was certain of that as well. Queen Mutnofret and Vizier Wersu would pretend they were pleased that he was well, but secretly they would still be plotting his death. He might not survive there for long.

He was getting used to the idea that he might die, but he hated the thought that his story would never be known. One evening after the day's work was over, Ramose decided to go for a walk up the mountain which rose up from the valley on the western side.

The peak of the mountain formed a natural pyramid shape. It was a sacred place known as the Gate of Heaven, which reached up to the sky and the realm of the gods. It was the home of the cobra goddess, Meretseger.

There were no paths leading up there. No one

ever climbed the Gate of Heaven, they had no reason to.

Ramose picked his way through the rocks and watched the workers' huts shrink and disappear into the sand as he climbed. He climbed up around the cliffs that surrounded the valley until he was higher than the rim of the Great Place. He could see over into the valley of the tomb makers' village and beyond that to the Nile Valley. If he squinted his eyes he could see a glint of white from the temples on the eastern bank of the river. He thought he might have seen a flash of gold from a flagpole. It was probably his imagination though. What he definitely could see was the sun getting lower in the sky. He would have to hurry.

After the suffocating tomb and the cramped and crowded hut, it was good to be alone and with space around him to breathe. He kept climbing. A vulture described slow, lazy circles above him. He came to a second cliff face. There was an untidy pile of twigs and dried grass perched on the top of it. It was the vulture's nest. He looked up at the great bird, symbol of the goddess Nekhbet, protector of the pharaoh. The bird must have flown many miles to bring the materials for its nest to this desert place. It was a good omen. He decided the place would suit his purposes well.

He unslung his reed bag and pulled out a copper chisel and a stone flake covered in his own untidy writing. He selected an area of the rock face, one that was set back in a fold of the cliff. For most of the day it would be in the narrow band of shade cast by the surrounding cliffs. At that time though, the rays of the setting sun shone onto it, burnishing it with an orange glow.

Before he set to work, Ramose said a short prayer to Thoth, the god of writing, and sprayed some drops of water on the cliff face. The text on the stone flake was the brief story of his escape from the palace. Now he was going to transcribe it onto the rock face. He got out his palette and a reed pen. First he marked vertical charcoal lines to help him keep the columns straight. Then, holding the stone flake in his left hand, he copied out the text in hieroglyphs. He wrote the words carefully in ink first.

In the eleventh year of the Pharaoh Tuthmosis, the first month of the season of peret, day seventeen, Prince Ramose, son of Pharaoh Tuthmosis and Queen Ahmose, beloved brother of Hatshepsut, lives. His enemies tried to end his life, but failed. Soon he will avenge their evil deeds. When his great father flies to heaven, Ramose will take his place as Pharaoh of Egypt.

The sun was getting low. Ra was about to start his perilous journey through the underworld

again. Before the sun rose again, the sun-god
would have to defeat the serpent-god, Apophis.
Ramose had to stop his work and get back to
the valley. He scrambled down the cliffs in the
gathering dark.

The next evening he returned and started to
carefully chisel out the hieroglyphs. He had little
experience at carving and it was slow work. He
wanted it to be neat. He carved each hieroglyph
with care. The work made him feel good. If Vizier
Wersu and Queen Mutnofret succeeded and killed
him, his story would be marked in stone forever.
Somewhere in the world the truth would be
written. Even if it was in a hidden fold of a cliff,
high in the hills, deep in the desert where no one
would ever see it.

He was concentrating hard, carving the first
column of hieroglyphs.

"Why do you come all the way up here to write?"
said a voice behind him.

Ramose nearly jumped out of his skin.

"Why do you go off climbing mountains in the
desert by yourself?"

"I wish you wouldn't follow me everywhere," he
said. It was Karoya, of course.

"Other Egyptians are afraid of the desert and
huddle together in their huts. You go marching
out into it alone."

"I don't like the desert any more than any other Egyptian. But I have a reason to be here."

Karoya looked at the hieroglyphs that Ramose had carved on the rock face.

"You could have carved pictures on rocks down in the valley."

"They aren't pictures. It's writing, the sort of writing used in the tombs. And I'm doing it up here because I don't want anyone to see it."

"What does it say?"

"It tells my story. If I die and never become pharaoh, it will be written here that I was betrayed."

"But no one will see it."

"Karoya, will you be quiet and let me work."

It took Ramose five visits to the cliff face to finish his carving. When he had carved the last hieroglyph, he washed off the ink and the charcoal markings and stood back to examine his work critically. He checked the hieroglyphs against his original writing on the stone flake to make sure he hadn't made any mistakes. Keneben would be proud of him, he thought. The hieroglyphs were well formed and even. The columns were straight. Perhaps even Paneb might have had a good word to say about his work.

It was getting late. The sun was about to sink below the horizon beyond the city. He hadn't stayed on the mountain so late before. Ramose picked up his tools and packed them into his reed bag. He heard a sound behind him, a movement of stones. He turned.

"Is that you, Karoya?" he said. "I told you not to follow me."

A figure came out of the growing shadows, and another. It wasn't Karoya who had followed him. A third figure emerged. It was Weni and his friends.

"What are you doing up here, scribbler?" asked Weni.

"I don't have to tell you why I do things."

"Why have you brought your scribe's tools up here?" Nakhtamun was looking around.

"What I do is none of your business."

"What's this?" said Hapu. He was stooping to pick up the stone flake.

"It's mine," Ramose grabbed at the stone flake and hurled it down into the valley. He could see it smash into pieces as it bounced down the rocky hill.

Weni moved closer to Ramose, looking around suspiciously. He scanned the ground and then the cliff face, now brilliant orange in the last rays of the sun. Another step and he would see the carving. Ramose stepped in front of him.

"Get out of the way," Weni snapped and pushed Ramose aside.

Ramose was still not used to being touched by people. He was suddenly the spoiled prince again, furious that a common labourer had dared to touch him. He flung out his hand in anger to stop Weni from touching him again. The back of his hand caught Weni in the face. His knuckles struck Weni's nose. Ramose turned to see Weni with his hand to his face and blood pouring between his fingers.

Now it was Weni's turn to be furious. Weni hated losing. He pushed Ramose again, harder. Ramose fell backwards, sprawled in the dust. Ramose leapt to his feet and launched himself at Weni. He grabbed him by the hair and kicked him in the shins. The two boys wrestled to the ground. There wasn't much room to move. Nakhtamun urged Weni on.

"Hit him. He deserves it!"

Ramose broke free from Weni's grip and got to his feet again.

"Be careful," cried Hapu. "You're near the edge."

All the anger that Ramose had kept under control for the past weeks burst forth. He threw himself at Weni, punching and kicking him. The boys wrestled to the ground, rolling dangerously close to the edge. Stones rattled down the hill into the growing darkness below. Weni got to his feet again. Ramose lunged at him. Weni hit out blindly in response. Ramose took a step back to avoid the blow. The ground beneath his foot crumbled and gave way. Ramose lost his balance and fell backwards. For a brief moment he saw the stunned faces of his three enemies staring down at him as he tumbled down the slope towards the cliff edge. He thought he saw a glint of triumph in Weni's eyes. Then their faces faded into darkness.

10

THE DESERT
AT NIGHT

RAMOSE AWOKE and shivered. He hoped it was a dream, but he was too scared to open his eyes. What if it wasn't? He opened one eye. It was dark. Ramose's body hurt. It hurt all over. His chest hurt most. His chest and his head. He could hear the scuffles of small creatures. He opened the other eye. He could see nothing but black. The goddess Meretseger's name meant "she who loves silence". She punished people who disturbed her peace by making them blind. Had the fight with Weni offended the cobra-goddess? He moved his head a fraction to the left. The black was now dotted with tiny pin points of light. The stars. The souls of the dead. He wasn't blind. He was cold though. The desert at night was very cold. Ramose had never felt so cold in his life. Something with a lot of legs walked slowly over his arm.

This was the third time he'd woken up and thought that he might be dead. This time he was pretty sure he wasn't. There were rocks sticking into his back. His right arm was up against earth. He reached out and could feel the rough rocky surface sloping up above him. He carefully moved his left hand. There was rock under his elbow, but further out he could feel nothing but cold air. He was on a ledge. Whether he was one cubit off the ground or a thousand, he had no way of telling. He was too scared to move. The ledge was narrow and he didn't want to fall again. He didn't think he could sit up anyway.

No one would come looking for him until morning and even then they might not bother. Would they take the workers away from building Pharaoh's tomb just to look for an apprentice scribe who had bad handwriting and a fear of enclosed spaces? He doubted that they would. He might be alive, but he didn't know for how long.

The moon slowly appeared above the starless black to his right. It was nearly full. With its light, Ramose could now see the shape of the rocky slope that he'd fallen down. The steeper cliff was below him. Ramose felt strangely at peace. Now that he was truly facing death he didn't feel afraid. He heard a howling in the distance. Hyenas. His heart suddenly leapt. His heart scarab was still in his reed bag up in the fold of cliff where he'd carved his story. When he reached the afterlife, how would Osiris know who he was? If the tomb makers buried him, the god of the underworld would think he was just an orphaned apprentice scribe. He would spend eternity as an apprentice scribe with no family.

A wave of loneliness washed over him. He wished he'd had a chance to see Hatshepsut again before he died. He had felt sad and lonely many times since that day in the palace when his pet monkey had died. If the truth was known, he was lonely even before then. But now he was completely alone. He was out in the desert, the land of the dead, far from the land of the living that clung to the Nile. A worse thought occurred to him. If no one found his body, he wouldn't go to the afterlife at all. His body would be eaten by vultures and hyenas. Then he would spend forever in oblivion.

Karoya might tell the tomb makers who he really was. They wouldn't believe her of course. She could take them to the carving he had made high in the cliffs of the Gate of Heaven. She might find his heart scarab so that it could be buried with him. He would have laughed if his chest wasn't hurting so much. His eternal salvation depended on a nosey, barbarian slave girl.

He drifted off to sleep and dreamt uncomfortable dreams of being lost in the underworld where even Topi the monkey didn't recognise him. He awoke again and the stars had moved. The moon was high above him. He was so cold he couldn't even move his fingers. The howl of the hyenas seemed closer.

There was one star that was crossing the sky so fast he could see it moving. It had a strange motion for a star. It seemed to be weaving back and forth in the sky. It was growing brighter. It was moving towards him. Perhaps Osiris knew he was about to die and was coming to get him. Perhaps he hadn't been abandoned after all.

"Ramose," said a voice. "Ramose, are you alive?" It was a female voice. Perhaps it was the cobra-goddess Meretseger come to lead him back up the mountain to heaven.

"I don't know," replied Ramose.

"I think we can assume you are," said another voice, a boy's voice.

The star lowered down to his face. It was an oil lamp in a hand. It was Karoya's hand. Her face came into the circle of light which made her black skin shine like polished ebony.

"Are you all right?" Another face came into the light. It was Hapu, the apprentice painter.

"Of course he isn't all right," said Karoya impatiently as she inspected Ramose in the lamplight. "He's covered in bruises and he's got a bad cut on his forehead."

She handed the lamp to Hapu and gently felt along Ramose's arms and legs. She held his head and moved it slowly to one side and then the other. She placed her hands on his chest. Ramose cried out in pain.

"You have some broken bones here," she said.

"We can't carry him," said Hapu.

"We don't have to carry him," replied Karoya. "He can walk."

Getting up and walking seemed like the most impossible thing in the world. Karoya pulled a leather pouch from her belt. She held it to Ramose's mouth. He felt liquid trickle down his throat. It wasn't water, it was wine. Ramose felt his insides warm. Karoya pulled a small metal box from the folds of her belt. Inside was something with a strong smell.

"What's that?" asked Ramose.

"Ointment from Kush. I only have a little left."

She rubbed the salve into Ramose's arms and legs. His limbs tingled and he could move his toes and fingers again.

"Hapu, you get behind him. We have to get him to his feet."

Hapu didn't know where to grip him. "I don't want to hurt him," he said.

"Sometimes pain can't be avoided," replied Karoya. "You push, I'll pull."

Ramose was thinking he was quite comfortable where he was, when an unbearably sharp pain in his chest made him cry out. Next thing he knew, he was on his feet.

The sky was starting to lighten. Ramose could now see that he had landed on a narrow ledge not much more than a cubit wide. If he had fallen any further, he would certainly have fallen to his death. Hapu was trying not to look at the sheer drop beneath them. It was a long way down.

"Let's get off this ledge."

"Can you walk, Ramose?"

Ramose nodded. His legs moved slowly and clumsily as if they were made of stone.

"I have your bag, Ramose," said Karoya. "We found it up higher where you and Weni fought."

She took Ramose's hand and led him slowly along the ledge until they came to a wider area that opened out and sloped down to the valley floor. Ramose had lost one of his sandals and the other one was broken. Hapu gave him his sandals to wear.

"I'm sorry we left you on the mountain," he said.

With Hapu supporting Ramose on one side and Karoya on the other, they made slow progress. Ramose learned that Weni and Nakhtamun had told no one about the incident on the mountain.

"I saw them follow you up the mountain," said Karoya. "Then I saw them return at nightfall without you."

She had confronted the boys, demanding to know what had happened. Weni and Nakhtamun wouldn't tell her, but Hapu had told her what had happened.

"Weni said we'd tell the foreman if you hadn't returned by daylight," Hapu told him. "I knew you could be dead by then."

They'd waited until the moon rose and then gone to look for him.

By the time they reached the safety of the valley floor it was daylight. Ra had survived his perilous night journey. So had Ramose.

11

PLACE OF BEAUTY

RAMOSE SCREWED up his nose. "What's that?" Karoya was pressing something soft, wet and foul-smelling against the wound on his head.

"It's meat."

"It smells awful."

"A wound on the head must be treated with a poultice of fresh meat on the first day."

"It doesn't smell fresh."

"It's as fresh as there is in this place."

"Is this another of your remedies from Kush?"

"No, I learnt this from an Egyptian priest." Karoya bound the meat to Ramose's forehead with a strip of linen. "Tomorrow I will just use oxen fat and honey."

"That sounds almost as bad," grumbled Ramose. "When I hurt myself back at the palace, priests said prayers over me and the royal jewellers made amulets to hang around my neck and ward off evil spirits."

"No priests. Just a piece of ox flesh."

"What about the broken bones in my chest?"

"They will heal as long as you rest."

Ramose didn't get to rest for long. He was given two days to recover before he was called before a special tribunal. Weni, Nakhtamun and Hapu were also summoned. The tribunal consisted of Scribe Paneb, Samut the foreman and two senior tomb workers.

"Why were you boys climbing the sacred mountain?" asked Paneb.

"We saw Ramose going up there and we were worried that he might get lost," Weni lied.

"And then when we found him, he just attacked Weni. He punched him in the nose," said Nakhtamun.

"Is this true, Ramose?" asked the foreman.

"I didn't mean to hit him," Ramose replied. "I just meant to push him away."

"I was just protecting myself," said Weni, "and then Ramose's foot slipped and he fell."

Hapu didn't say anything.

"You have behaved irresponsibly," said Paneb.

"We are all here at the Great Place to prepare the tomb of the pharaoh, may he have long life and health," said the foreman. "You striplings are privileged to work in this place. You have been trusted with knowledge of the whereabouts of Pharaoh's tomb. Only we tomb workers know this. The Great Place and the Gate of Heaven are sacred places."

"You should be banished from the Great Place," said Paneb. "But with two tombs now under construction we need all the workers we can get."

It was agreed that each boy should receive ten blows and pay a fine of a week's grain ration. Ramose was exempted from the beating, as he was already covered with purple and yellow bruises.

"I think it would be a good idea to separate you boys for a while," said Samut. "Ramose and Hapu, you can go to the Place of Beauty. Report to the foreman there tomorrow morning."

The Place of Beauty was the valley to the south of the Great Place. It was meant for the burial of other members of the royal family. There were three tombs there. Two belonged to Ramose's brothers, Wadzmose and Amenmose. The entrances to those tombs were hidden so that tomb robbers couldn't find them. Ramose found himself at the entrance of the third tomb in the Place of Beauty, which was still under construction. It was his own tomb.

Ramose had been so busy in the Great Place, concerned with daily life, the possibility of death and the sharpness of chisels, that he hadn't had time to think about the preparations for his own burial. The mood of the workers at this tomb was completely different to that of the men working on Pharaoh's tomb. Men were hurrying about. There was a sense of urgency. The moment the two boys arrived, the foreman put them to work. He sent Hapu down into the tomb to help the painters.

"I want you to check the script on the tomb walls," the foreman told Ramose. "This has been a rushed job and our scribe has been ill for weeks. Check for mistakes."

Ramose entered the tomb and the cool air gave him goose bumps. It was a small tomb compared to his father's. A few steps led down to a short corridor, which opened straight into the burial chamber. The chamber was a strange shape. Instead of being rectangular, it was narrow at one end. One corner had an ugly, jagged lump sticking out of it. The foreman saw Ramose looking at it.

"The quarry men ran into a flint boulder in the rock," he explained. The rock deep in the desert hills was generally quite soft and easy to carve, but occasionally there were outcrops of hard flint. The tomb makers' copper chisels buckled and broke when they hit flint.

"We didn't have time to start a new excavation, so we had to leave it. It'll make it difficult to fit the sarcophagus in, but it can't be helped."

Ramose looked at the artwork on the walls. A team of six painters, now including Hapu, were painting texts on three of the walls. They were instructions for how to travel through the dangerous underworld. The painters were also drawing maps showing two different ways to get past the monsters and lakes of fire. Hapu was on his knees, painting a border of papyrus reeds and Horus eyes.

"We've only had time to carve sculptures on one of the walls," said the foreman.

"Will there be no carvings in the corridor?

"No, there isn't time."

Ramose opened his mouth to complain.

"It's not my fault the royal princes keep dying so young," grumbled the foreman. "Three tombs in two years! How are we supposed to cope?"

Ramose looked closer at a half-finished carving

of Anubis, the jackal-headed god of the dead, leading a young boy into the presence of Osiris, the god of the underworld. A sculptor was gently chipping away at the rock to shape the boy's kilt. Another sculptor was carving the boy's name alongside in elegant hieroglyphs. It was Ramose's name.

Ramose realised that the carving was of himself. His heart was being weighed against the feather of truth. Thoth, the ibis-headed god of writing, was noting down the results. The monster Ammut, part crocodile, part lion, part hippopotamus watched, ready to pounce on the heart and devour it if it was heavy with wrong-doing.

Another sculptor was working on the other end of the wall. He was putting the finishing touches to a carving of Ramose's family: Pharaoh, his mother, his beautiful sister Hatshepsut, his two brothers and himself as a small boy. He was sitting on his mother's lap. A cat was playing under her chair.

It probably wasn't a real likeness of his mother. The man who had drawn the outline for the sculptor would never have seen her. Ramose couldn't remember what she looked like. He held a lamp up to the image of his mother's face. It was beautiful. Calm and smiling. One elegant hand was resting on the shoulder of the child on her lap. Another sculptor, who was working on the hieroglyphs, had finished his work on the other carving. He came over and started to carve the names of the family members. He was a skilled craftsman. Following the outlines painted on the walls, he carved the shapes with smooth assured strokes. The hastily drawn outlines were transformed into neat three-dimensional hieroglyphs, each one a small work of art.

Ramose looked closer. Next to the image of his mother the sculptor had carved the hieroglyphs for Mutnofret.

"Stop!" Ramose reached out and grabbed hold of the sculptor's hand.

"What do you think you're doing, stripling?" said the sculptor.

"You've made a mistake," said Ramose angrily.

The sculptor turned to look at the new apprentice scribe, surprised by the tone of his voice. "What are you talking about?"

"Mutnofret is only a lesser queen. The name of the Great Royal Wife was Ahmose. You've carved the wrong name."

"We're in a hurry," the sculptor said, going back to his carving. "I haven't got time to redo it."

"You have to change it," shouted Ramose as he prised the chisel from the sculptor's hand.

Hapu looked over to see his new friend grappling with the sculptor. He ran across to restrain Ramose before he got hurt in the scuffle.

"Calm down, Ramose. Does it matter if it's the wrong queen?"

"Yes it does matter. It matters a lot. Mutnofret isn't the Prince Ramose's mother. It has to be changed."

Ramose stopped struggling and Hapu released his hold. As soon as he was free, Ramose lunged at the sculpture and with the chisel attacked the name of the hated queen. He gouged the first two hieroglyphs from the wall before the startled tomb workers realised what he was doing and wrestled him to the floor. Ramose fell hard and cried out in pain as his unhealed ribs hit the stone floor.

Hapu pushed through the knot of men around his friend and knelt at his side.

"He's still recovering from an accident," Hapu pointed to the gash on the side of Ramose's head. "He fell. It's affected his judgment a little."

"A lot, I'd say," said the sculptor looking at the damage done to his work.

The foreman came into the burial chamber.

"What's all the noise about?"

"This new apprentice scribe is gouging holes in the walls."

"It was wrong," said Ramose holding his chest. "I just wanted the queen's name to be right. You told me to check for mistakes."

"I didn't tell you to gouge holes anywhere."

The men looked at the apprentice scribe and

shook their heads as they went back to their work. Ramose took a stone flake and a pen from his bag. He wrote his mother's name on it as neatly as he could.

"This is the real queen's name," he said, handing it to the sculptor.

"Plaster over the damage," said the foreman, "and recarve the queen's name." He turned to Ramose. "You," he said angrily. "Go and check the painted hieroglyphs on the other walls, that's what you're here to do."

Ramose and Hapu ate their midday meal out in the valley. "You must like getting into trouble," Hapu said with a wry smile.

"Of course I don't."

"You wouldn't think so," said Hapu through a mouthful of dried fish. "We've only been here for one morning and you've already upset half the team and been fined a sack of grain for damaging the tomb."

Ramose dipped bread into his lentil soup, and ate it without commenting.

"You're a strange person." Hapu looked at Ramose, trying to work out his new friend.

"What's strange about me?"

"You climb mountains by yourself, you attack tomb carvings, you have a slave for a friend."

"I have good reasons for all of those things."

"I'm sure you do, but I don't know what they are."

"I can't explain."

"Perhaps it's because you come from the south."

"Maybe." Ramose was keen to change the topic of conversation. "Do you miss your friends?" he asked Hapu.

"Not much. Weni isn't really my friend. He's a troublemaker."

"Like me."

"No, not like you. Weni's mean. He likes to hurt people. You don't get into trouble on purpose." Hapu laughed. "You're not mean, you're just not very smart."

Ramose laughed too. A few weeks ago, if anyone had made fun of him in that way, he would have been angry. Now he didn't mind.

"Come on, you boys," said the foreman as he passed by them in a hurry. "Time to get back to work. A messenger just came up from the city. There's going to be a royal visit."

"The pharaoh?" asked Hapu. "He's coming here?"

"That's right, Pharaoh himself, may he have long life, health and prosperity. He'll be here in a few days to see how his tomb's progressing. Half our team will have to go down to the village to get his residence in shape."

"Will he be coming to inspect the prince's tomb as well?" asked Ramose.

"Yes, and we have orders to finish it before he does."

Ramose's heart started thudding. He didn't have to worry about how he could get into the palace to see his father. His father was coming to him. This was Ramose's chance. He could see his father and let him know that he was still alive.

12

ROYAL VISIT

THE TOMB WORKERS spent the next nine days working very long hours to get the tomb finished. There wasn't really enough time, but they did their best to have the tomb as close to finished as they could. Ramose was grateful to them for this, even though it wasn't him that was going to be buried there. He checked the texts on the walls carefully. The peasant boy who was to be buried there in his place deserved to find his way safely through the underworld.

At the end of the shift there was a feast to celebrate the completion of the tomb and to thank the workers for their hard work. Extra food was released from the tomb stores and special bread and cakes were baked. There was to be a holiday as well. Instead of the usual two days break, the workers had four days before they had to report back to duty at the Great Place.

Ramose and Hapu walked wearily up the path. When they reached the top of the hill, they could see the village below them. Usually there was no sign of activity and the mud brick village could easily have been mistaken for part of the landscape. Now people were running around between the village and the dusty mud brick building which stood outside the village walls. The building had been half-finished the whole time Ramose had been in the valley.

In their absence, it had been hastily transformed into a royal residence. Its walls were now finished. The end wall had darker patches where the fresh mud bricks hadn't quite dried. The other walls were being whitewashed. Men were clearing rocks from around the building and levelling a path branching off from the one that came down the opposite hill from the city. Other men were erecting two gold-tipped flagpoles just like the ones that circled the palace on the banks of the Nile. A dozen donkeys stood outside the building. People hurried back and forth unloading piles of furniture and food from the donkeys' backs.

Karoya was waiting at the village gate for them.

"You've heard the news I suppose?" she asked as they approached.

"About Pharaoh's visit?" said Hapu. "Of course we've heard. We had to get the prince's tomb ready for inspection."

"The donkeys have been coming and going all day. I've never seen such things. Look at that furniture!"

Chairs and low tables were being carried into the residence. Each item was painted in bright colours or inlaid with gold and turquoise and lapis lazuli. There were also three gold-painted couches carved in the shape of animals: a lion, a leopard, a gazelle.

Karoya looked at Ramose. He hadn't said a word. She knew what this meant for him.

Hapu was chatting on, unaware. "We had a feast in the Valley, with wine and sweet cakes," he said. "Didn't you save a cake for Karoya, Ramose?"

Ramose nodded and pulled a linen package from his bag and handed it to Karoya. She unwrapped the present and smiled. It was a cake in the shape of a cat.

"What will we do for four days?" Hapu asked as they walked into the village.

"I have a few ideas," said Ramose.

The next morning the scene outside the village hardly seemed to have changed. More donkeys were arriving laden with goods for the royal residence. Ramose and his friends were all called on to help with the work. Holiday or not, everyone had to make sure everything was ready for Pharaoh.

In the afternoon, ignoring the heat of the sun, the entire population of the village gathered outside to welcome their pharaoh. Few of them had ever seen him before. They waited and waited. Ramose stood nervously among the crowd. They waited some more.

"Why have you brought your palette and pen?" asked Hapu.

"I might be needed to record something," said Ramose vaguely.

Karoya guessed he had a plan, but she didn't know what it was.

Eventually a party of about twenty people on foot appeared over the rim of the valley.

"There are so many of them," said Karoya who was standing upon a rock so she could get a better view. "I wonder which one of them is Pharaoh?"

Hapu laughed.

"None of them. They're all servants, musicians, dancers, cooks."

Two covered chairs appeared on the path. They were draped with white cloth edged in gold and carried on poles by more servants.

"That's Pharaoh," said Hapu.

"But he's covered up. I won't be able to see him," said Karoya disappointed.

"You'll be in his presence, that's enough."

"Who is in the other covered box?" asked Karoya, craning her neck still hoping to get a glimpse.

"I don't know," said Ramose. "Probably Queen Mutnofret."

Ramose knew that if he was going to act, it had to be now. While his friends were peering at the royal procession, he moved towards the workers who were frantically carrying in the last of the food supplies. Four donkeys were still waiting patiently as they were unloaded. The gateway to the royal residence was guarded by two men armed with daggers. Ramose walked up to the donkeys and whacked one of them on the rump. The startled animal took off at great speed, trampling through a pile of vegetables. The other donkeys galloped after it.

"Quick," shouted Ramose to the guards. "Catch those animals. Pharaoh approaches. He'll be here in a matter of minutes."

The guards obediently ran after the donkeys.

Ramose pulled out his scribe's palette and a stone flake and pretended to jot down some notes. He picked up a basket of onions and walked in through the gate.

His plan was hazy. He didn't want to present himself to his father in a crowd of people. It would be a shock, after all his father thought he was dead. What he wanted to do was hide somewhere and go to his father when he was alone in his private chamber. The courtyard was a frenzy of last minute activity. Ramose strode through it and into the residence as if he belonged there. He did belong there.

People were rushing around inside as well. Ramose marched down the corridor purposefully, carrying his palette and with a reed pen pushed behind his ear. No one questioned him.

Two chambers had been prepared. One was full of women arranging mirrors, cosmetics and draperies around a bed. He glimpsed the golden animal-shaped couches. The chamber opposite had a larger bed with a carved wooden canopy and a beautiful gilt chair decorated with carved lions' heads and with winged serpents as armrests. Ramose entered the room. Light from the lowering sun slanted in through grilles in the ceiling and lit up the rich fabric on the bed. He sniffed the cool air, which was sweet with frankincense. Off the main room was a smaller room with a white alabaster bath sunk into the floor. Large clay water jars, almost as tall as Ramose, stood next to the bath. The jars were full of fresh water to pour over Pharaoh. It was Nile water carried all the way up from the river valley.

The voices and running feet in the residence suddenly fell silent. Ramose knew the royal procession had arrived. He stayed in the bathing room and waited. His heart was beating so loud that it seemed to fill the silent room. He was going to see his father. He only had to wait a few minutes, but it seemed like a long, long time. Then he heard a deep voice rasp out orders in the outer chamber.

"Where is my clean clothing? Bring me some wine at once."

The voice was familiar. It was a voice he'd known all his life. But it wasn't his father's. It was the impatient, angry voice of Vizier Wersu.

"I want to get out of these dirty clothes and wash off the dust from this wretched place."

Ramose looked around. There was nowhere to hide. He heard servants rush in with the vizier's clothes chest. He heard footsteps approaching. Ramose knew that if the vizier saw him he would be dead before the end of day. He had no choice. There was only one place to hide. Ramose hoisted himself up and into one of the huge water jars. The cold water took his breath away. As he lowered his body into the jar, the water overflowed onto the white stone floor. The water level was right at the lip of the jar. Ramose's head was still in full view. The footsteps grew louder. Ramose closed his eyes and ducked his head under the water. With his head tipped back, he could just manage to hold his nose above the surface.

The vizier came into the room. From under the water, Ramose could hear the distorted sounds of his crocodile voice shouting at the servants. Even though there was two finger-widths of clay between them, Ramose felt exposed. He'd always had the feeling that Wersu could see through walls. He was terrified that the vizier would discover him. He closed his eyes.

All the time he'd been in the desert, Ramose had dreamt of immersing his body in the waters of the Nile, of feeling its coolness and smelling the humid air around it. This wasn't what he'd had in mind. He felt trapped. He tried to imagine that he was floating in the Nile instead. That he wasn't cramped in a water jar like a mummy in a coffin. He sucked long deep breaths of air through his nose to calm him. I am in the river, he told himself. I am drifting in the river among lotus flowers and fish. Hopefully the servants would use the other jar to get water to bathe the vizier.

Ramose could hear footsteps echoing hollowly outside the jar. A dull clunk of something banging against the clay made him jump. He opened his eyes. A hand swam into view above him holding a large copper dipper. Ramose took a deep breath and pulled his head right under the water, crouching down inside the jar. The dipper plunged into the water above his head. It seemed to take an age for it to fill and then to be lifted out again. Finally it disappeared from sight. Ramose raised his head.

As his nose broke clear of the surface, in his hunger for air, he breathed in water. He spluttered and water filled his mouth and nose. He pushed his head right out of the jar alternately coughing and greedily gulping in air. Fortunately the vizier was facing away from the jar and loudly complaining about the lack of cleansing oils in this makeshift place. His servant was concentrating on pouring the water over the vizier's head. Neither of them heard or saw Ramose.

The dipper plunged in another ten or more times, and each time the water level fell until Ramose could crouch in the jar's depths with his head clear of the water.

When Vizier Wersu had finished bathing, Ramose waited until the outer chamber was silent again. He climbed out of the jar and dripped into the other room. He slumped down on the gilt chair with the lion head decorations and the winged serpent armrests. Now that he could breathe easy again, he had time to feel bitter disappointment. His father wasn't in the inspection party. Only two rooms had been prepared, this one and the one opposite which was obviously arranged for a woman. He had thought that his ordeal was over, and it wasn't. His father was as far away as ever. His plan was ruined.

He heard more footsteps approaching, the crash of a dropped tray and angry muttered words. He didn't move. He didn't care if he was discovered in the vizier's rooms. A face peered around the doorway, a dark face framed by a twist of red and green material. It was Karoya. She slipped into the room noiselessly. There was another crash and Hapu stumbled into the room carrying a large copper platter of jumbled fruit.

"Your friend is as stealthy as an elephant," whispered Karoya angrily to Ramose. She glared at Hapu. "I told you not to follow me."

Hapu was not normally clumsy, but it was obvious from his face that he was very nervous. "We could be put to death for this," he said. "What are you doing here, Ramose?"

"It's a long story," sighed Ramose.

"Get up off that chair! You'll damage it, dripping on it like that. The gold paint will peel off."

Ramose took no notice of him.

"Pharaoh isn't here," said Karoya.

"I know."

There was despair in Ramose's voice.

"I don't understand why you came in here at all," said Hapu. "It's just as if you are looking for trouble."

"I'm not looking for trouble."

"Well let's get out of here then, before anyone comes."

Ramose didn't move. Karoya grabbed him by the arm.

"Come on, Ramose," she said.

She dragged Ramose to his feet and peered around the door frame. "There's no one around."

She crept out into the corridor still holding on to Ramose.

"Bring the tray," she ordered Hapu. "In case we run into anyone."

They had no sooner stepped through the doorway into the corridor than laughter could be heard from someone approaching. A group of women rounded the corner chattering and laughing. They were like a vision, all wearing flowing white gowns and jewellery. The smell of perfume filled the corridor. Karoya froze.

"Keep walking," whispered Hapu. "Don't look at them."

Karoya did as Hapu said, pulling Ramose behind her. They passed the laughing women with bowed heads and purposeful steps. One of the women spoke just as they passed them.

"I hope they brought some gazelle milk up from the valley," she said.

Ramose stopped dead and turned towards the woman.

"Hatshepsut!"

13

GIFTS FROM A PRINCESS

"**W**HO CALLS Princess Hatshepsut's name?" demanded one of the women.

"Ramose, now what are you doing?" whispered Hapu unable to believe his friend was looking for more trouble. "What's wrong with you? We were almost out of here."

Ramose didn't hear either of them. He was

staring at his sister. It was only just over two months since Ramose had seen her, but she had changed in that short time. She had lost her girlishness and become a young woman. He felt a rush of jumbled emotions: love, pride, homesickness. Karoya stood with her mouth open, staring at the beautiful princess.

Hatshepsut had a dazzling white gown that fell from her waist in finely pressed pleats. Around her neck was a deep collar made of gold with thousands of semi-precious stone making up a wonderful design of lotus flowers. She had matching armbands and earrings. She was wearing a wig divided into hundreds of tiny plaits, each one ending in a gold bead in the shape of a cowry shell. On top of it was a gold crown with a rearing snake's head on it. Her eyes were lined with kohl and her eyelids painted a shimmering green. She looked like a goddess.

Hapu didn't know what to do in front of such a vision so he fell to his knees and bowed down before her. Ramose stood smiling at his sister, he reached out to make sure she was real. Hatshepsut pulled her arm away before he could touch her. Her four companions drew around their mistress as if she might be contaminated by closeness to such an inferior person.

"What is it that you want, servant?" asked Hatshepsut. Her voice was like music from a lute.

"Why are you in this part of the residence? Only my personal maids and the vizier's servants are permitted in here."

Karoya just kept staring. Hapu tried to speak but failed. Ramose's smile faded. He realised that his sister didn't know who he was.

"Penu," he said. "Don't you recognise me? It's Ramose."

Hatshepsut turned and studied his face.

"Ramose?" she said.

"Your brother."

The calm, self-confident look on the princess's face faded as she stared at the wet-haired boy in the stained kilt. She changed before his eyes from a composed princess to a confused young girl. She peered into his face.

"Ramose?"

"You've changed so much in such a short time. Have I changed too?"

Hatshepsut reached out and pushed a lock of wet hair back from his face and touched the scar on his forehead.

"Is it really you, Ramose?"

Ramose nodded. "It's me, Penu."

Hatshepsut put her arms around her brother. Ramose felt her wet cheek brush his as he hugged her. He wanted to cry out with happiness. He had his sister back.

In Hatshepsut's chamber, Ramose sat next to

her on the golden gazelle-shaped couch and told her his story. He told her about his faked death, his escape to the tomb makers' village and how the banishment of Keneben his tutor had cut off his only link with the palace. He told her how much he'd missed her. Hapu sat with his mouth open as he heard the story for the first time. Hatshepsut listened, her face pale with shock.

"You've been very brave," she said when he finished. "Father would be proud of you."

"I thought that Father was going to be in the inspection party," Ramose said.

"He isn't well. I took his place at the last minute." Hatshepsut's face clouded with sadness. "He became ill while he was in Kush." The princess glanced at Karoya.

"I have to see him," said Ramose. "I have to let him know that I'm still alive."

"I don't think it would be a good time to go back," said Hatshepsut. "Mutnofret is even more powerful now. She acts as if her brat is already pharaoh. She and Wersu are acting together as co-regents. Father is too ill to realise what she's doing."

"What do you want me to do? Stay here for- ever?"

"No, of course not," said Hatshepsut taking her brother's hand. "Just wait. Wait until father is strong again. I'll arrange for Keneben to be sent back to Thebes. I'll send you word when it's safe to come, when Wersu and Mutnofret are away from the palace. It won't be long, I promise."

"I want to go home, Penu." Ramose felt tears well in his eyes. He couldn't help it. The memories of home flooded back.

Hatshepsut reached out and hugged him again.

"I can't imagine what it's been like for you, living as you have and being all alone."

"I haven't been alone," he said, turning to Karoya and Hapu.

As soon as the princess looked at Hapu, he fell to his knees again.

"This is Hapu," said Ramose. "He's an apprentice painter in the Great Place. We've been working together there on Father's tomb. He's become a good friend."

Hatshepsut smiled. "He seems rather stunned by these events."

"He's only just found out who I am."

He turned to Karoya. "And this is Karoya. She's a slave from Kush who grinds grain for the scribe."

"A slave? You have a strange collection of friends, Ramose."

"Karoya saved my life."

"The slave girl doesn't seem surprised to know who you are."

"I told her some time ago. She had already half guessed, anyway."

"A very clever slave it would seem."

"A very inquisitive slave," replied Ramose smiling at Karoya.

Hatshepsut had regained her composure. She looked and sounded like a princess again.

"Here," she said taking off one of her bracelets and handing it to Karoya. "A reward for taking care of my brother. I suspect he's needed some help."

"I don't need a reward," said Karoya looking the princess in the eye.

"Then take it as a gift from me."

Karoya took the bracelet from the princess, turning it over in her hands so that it caught the rays of sun that were angling in through the grilles in the ceiling.

Hatshepsut looked down at Hapu who was still on his knees.

"Stand up," she said touching him on the head.

Hapu stood up, blushing under the princess' gaze. "I'd like to thank you as well for helping my brother." She went over to a chest and opened the lid. It was full of jewellery.

Karoya stared at the chest. "I've never seen so much gold and jewels," she said.

"This is just my travelling chest," said Hatshepsut reaching into the chest.

She pulled out a small amulet on a gold chain.

"Here," she said. "Take this. It's in the shape of the knot of Isis, so that the goddess will watch over you."

Hapu took the amulet in his hand. It was made of red jasper and finely carved with papyrus reeds. He opened his mouth to thank the princess, but his voice failed him again. Princess Hatshepsut smiled at the apprentice painter, aware of the effect she was having on him. She turned to Ramose.

"There is a banquet I must attend. Wersu will be wondering where I am."

Ramose glanced at the women. "Can we trust them?"

"Yes. They'll do whatever I ask them," said Hatshepsut. "I'll send one of them with you to the gate, so that I know you got away safely."

Ramose hugged his sister, clinging onto her, not wanting her to go. She pulled herself gently away. Ramose watched her as she swept out of the rooms. Part of him would have given anything to follow her and step back into his old life again. Another part of him knew he had to follow through what he'd started. He turned back to his friends.

"She's…" said Hapu. It was all he could manage to say.

Ramose smiled. "We'd better get out of here," he said. He led his friends down the corridor.

When they reached the courtyard, they were surprised to find it was almost dark. They were more surprised to find six royal guards barring their way with long-handled spears. A tall, thin figure in a long robe stepped out of the shadows. He was holding a lamp in insect-like hands. It was Vizier Wersu.

The lamplight threw sharp shadows on his crocodile face. Behind him were two smaller figures dressed in the working kilts of the tomb makers: Weni and Nakhtamun.

Ramose hung back in the shadows behind Karoya where the vizier couldn't see his face.

"Search them," ordered Wersu. Three guards stepped forward and grabbed Ramose and his friends.

"Take your hands off me," yelled Karoya punching the guard as he tried to search through the folds of her belt. He found the princess's bracelet and held it up.

The guard holding Hapu easily found the amulet that the princess had given him.

"See, I told you they'd come into the royal residence to steal," said Nakhtamun triumphantly.

"I can't find anything on this one, sir," said the guard searching Ramose. "Wait a minute, bring over the light."

The vizier strode over towards Ramose.

"He's got something in his hand."

The guard grabbed Ramose's hand and roughly prised open his fingers. In the palm of his hand was his heart scarab. The lamplight illuminated the blue and gold of the scarab and a trick of the light made it look huge.

"It's a heart scarab," said the vizier, moving his lamp closer to the jewel in Ramose's hand. "A royal one by the look of it."

"He's a tomb robber!" cried Weni. "I knew he was up to something."

Ramose turned his head away, afraid that the vizier would recognise him.

"He's not a tomb robber," cried Hapu. "You don't know who you've got there."

The vizier turned to Hapu.

"You'll be very sorry you did this, Weni," continued Hapu. "Ramose is no thief, he's—"

"Someone I summoned to the residence," said a calm voice behind them.

Everyone turned and saw Princess Hatshepsut drifting toward them in the light of four lamps held by her female companions. The circle of light only reached as far as her knees, giving the illusion that she was floating above the ground. The red eyes in the snake's head on her crown flashed.

"I thought it would be amusing to meet some people my own age who live and work out here in the desert," said Hatshepsut looking Vizier

Wersu square in the eye. "Why are you holding my guests at the point of a spear?"

"I have been informed that they are thieves," said the vizier. "The slave girl has what looks to be one of your bracelets, Highness."

"It was a gift from me, as was the amulet that I gave to the young man who blushes easily."

Hapu blushed again.

"What about the heart scarab? Surely that has been stolen from a tomb."

Ramose glanced at his sister. She wouldn't be able to explain away the scarab so easily. Her face was as calm as ever.

"Really, Vizier Wersu," said Hatshepsut with a laugh. "Can't you tell a real lapis lazuli scarab from the painted ceramic copies that can be bought at any market stall in the city?"

The vizier peered at the stone in the dim light. Ramose kept his head turned away and his heart scarab firmly in his hand.

"Now, Vizier," continued Hatshepsut. "If you've finished, I think you have kept the tomb officials waiting long enough. They are wondering where you are."

Vizier Wersu was angry at being made to look foolish. "I'll see that you boys receive ten lashes and a fine of a month's wages for this," he said glaring at Weni and Nakhtamun.

Hatshepsut turned and drifted serenely back

into the royal residence in the halo of light provided by her companions.

"Come along, Vizier," she said.

The vizier dismissed the guards with a jerk of his head and followed the princess. The guards escorted Weni and Nakhtamun out. Ramose watched his sister until she was out of sight. Hapu turned to Ramose.

"Why didn't you tell me you were a prince?" said Hapu. "Didn't you trust me to keep your secret?"

"It had nothing to do with trust," said Ramose. "It's dangerous knowledge. I didn't want to put you at risk."

Hapu looked at his friend with confusion. "I don't know how to speak to you any more."

"Speak to him the same as you always have," exclaimed Karoya. "He's the same person he was when you thought he was an apprentice scribe."

Hapu didn't look convinced.

"She's right," said Ramose. "When I first came here I was a spoilt prince. I think I've changed."

"Oh," said Karoya, "and what are you now?"

Ramose thought for a moment. "I'm still a prince," he said. "But now I'm a prince who knows what it's like to get dirt under his fingernails."

Karoya laughed.

Ramose was standing on a dry, rocky hill. He looked around. There wasn't a blade of anything growing. He looked down at himself. His clothes were dusty and his reed sandals were worn. He knew exactly where the remains of his red leather sandals were, the ones with the turned-up toes: they had been thrown into the rubbish pit outside the tomb makers' village weeks ago.

He heard a mournful chanting drifting up from below. Snaking along in the valley was a procession. At the front was a jackal-headed priest. The sun reflected on gold and jewels. A beautiful coffin on an ornate sled was being pulled by six oxen. Six priests followed behind. They all wore brilliant white robes with leopard skins draped over their shoulders. It was a funeral procession. Ramose looked closer. How many loads of funeral goods were there? How many mourners were there?

He had a special interest in this funeral.

It was his own.

It was just like his dream seventy days ago, except this time he knew for sure it wasn't a dream and he knew that he wasn't dead.

"Look!" he said to Hapu. "That's my funeral."

Hapu smiled awkwardly. He was still getting used to the fact that his friend was a prince. "It looks impressive. Nicely painted sleds and tomb furniture from what I can see."

Karoya was standing on his left, with the length of red and green cloth wrapped over her head to shield her from the sun. The princess's gift glinted on her arm. "A lot of fuss for a clumsy apprentice scribe, I'd say."

Ramose smiled at his friends. That was why he knew he wasn't dreaming. In his dream he'd been alone and frightened in a strange place. Now he knew where he was, he knew where he was going and he had the company of friends.

He looked back over the desert hills to the green Nile valley and the silver strip of the river. Somewhere within the whitewashed walls beside the river, below the pennants fluttering from gold-tipped flagpoles, was his sister. That was where his future lay, over there in the palace on the banks of the beautiful river. But for now he had a life over the next hill in the Great Place, another shift to work. He turned back to the path.

A WORD FROM THE AUTHOR

THE HISTORY of the ancient Egyptians spans a period of three thousand years from around 3000 BC to 30 BC. They lived a long time ago, but we have lots of information about them. One reason for this is because of the tombs they built to preserve the bodies of pharaohs. The tombs contained all the everyday things they needed in the afterlife, such as furniture, cooking pots and clothing. The walls of the tombs were decorated with pictures of daily life. The tombs have been robbed or destroyed over the millennia, but there is still enough remaining to tell us a lot about the way Egyptians lived.

The other reason we know so much about ancient Egyptian life is that the Egyptians liked writing. They kept records of everything they did. Near the village of the tomb workers, in the area now known as the Valley of the Kings, archaeologists found a rubbish pit filled with thousands of stone chips, all covered with writing. From these chips we have learnt an amazing amount of detail about the lives of these ordinary people: what they ate, what they were paid, arguments they had with each other. Reading about the lives of these workers who died more than two thousand years ago inspired me to write a story set in ancient Egypt.

RAMOSE

RAMOSE AND THE TOMB ROBBERS

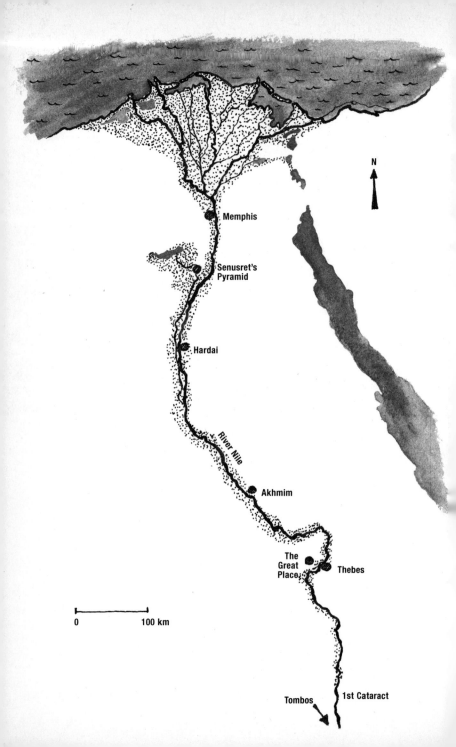

N

Memphis

Senusret's
Pyramid

Hardai

River Nile

Akhmim

The
Great
Place

Thebes

0   100 km

Tombos   1st Cataract

1

IBIS EGGS AND HONEY CAKES

"I WANT a cat," said Karoya.

"What for?" Ramose was sitting in the garden eating breakfast.

The small square of sunbaked sand at the back of Scribe Paneb's house, where Ramose and Karoya lived, hardly deserved to be called a garden. It was really an outdoor kitchen. The only things growing there were a struggling row

of onions and a few herbs. The rest of the garden
was just dry trodden earth. In one corner was
the conical oven where Karoya baked bread for
the household and the curved stone on which
she ground grain every day. That's what Karoya
was doing as Ramose watched her. She was on
her hands and knees rolling a smooth round
stone over the wheat grains that were sprinkled
on the curved grinding stone. It was hard work.
Karoya sat up on her heels to rest for a moment.
She wiped her sweating brow on a fold of the red
and green striped length of cloth that she wore
draped over her head and massaged her back
with her fingertips. Ramose would have liked to
help her with her work, but Karoya was a slave.
It wouldn't have been right for him to do a slave's
work.

"A cat would eat the mice," replied Karoya.
"Stop them from ruining the grain."

"You just want a pet," smiled Ramose.

"I do not! It would scare away snakes."

"We've managed without a cat before," said
Ramose. "Why do you suddenly need one?"

Karoya went back to her grinding. After a
while she spoke again. "It would be nice to have
something that is just mine."

It was the first time Ramose had ever heard
Karoya wish for anything. She was the property
of Pharaoh, taken from her homeland of Kush

and brought to Egypt to work as a slave. She owned nothing but the clothes she wore.

"I suppose Prince Ramose had dozens of cats back at the palace," said Karoya sulkily.

Ramose looked around anxiously. "Sssh. Don't ever call me that. Someone might hear."

"Well did you?"

"There were several cats, yes. But I had a pet monkey."

Karoya didn't look impressed.

"Where I come from there are lots of monkeys. They are a nuisance. They eat the dates and steal food. People chase them away. There are no cats though."

Ramose's monkey had come from Kush as well. Like Karoya, the monkey had been taken from the land of Kush because it suited Pharaoh. The life Ramose had lived as a prince seemed so long ago it was like another lifetime. Actually it wasn't long ago at all. Only eight months earlier his home had been the palace in the city.

For all of his eleven years he had lived the pampered life of Pharaoh's son, heir to the throne of Egypt. He had been a different person then, spoilt and thoughtless, taking everything for granted. He'd had no worries—and he certainly hadn't had a slave for a friend. Things had changed since then.

Ramose's tutor, Keneben, and Heria, his beloved

nanny, had been sure that Queen Mutnofret was trying to kill him. She was one of Pharaoh's lesser wives and she wanted her own son to be the next pharaoh. Ramose's two older brothers had already died. Keneben and Heria believed that Mutnofret had killed the older princes. They had begun testing Ramose's food on his pet monkey. Ramose knew nothing about this until the day he'd found his monkey dead.

Keneben and Heria had faked Ramose's death and sent him into hiding for safety. He was now living in secret as an apprentice scribe in the Great Place, the desert valley that his father had chosen as the place for his own tomb and the tombs of all future pharaohs.

At first he'd been comforted to know that he had friends at the palace. Then his nanny had died and Queen Mutnofret had sent Keneben to a foreign land. Ramose was on his own now. Only his sister, Hatshepsut, knew he was still alive and that one day he intended to be pharaoh.

His past and his future both seemed very distant. At the moment Ramose had to deal with his present life. He worked eight-day shifts at the tomb site along with the sculptors, painters and quarry men who were constructing his father's tomb. He had just finished his two-day break and was about to return to the tomb for another shift.

"I better get going," said Ramose finishing the last of his figs.

"I'll see you when I come up to the Great Place," said Karoya. She had to grind grain and do other work at the tomb site.

Ramose walked through the house. The scribe was still eating his breakfast.

"I'll go on ahead, Paneb," Ramose said.

The scribe said something with his mouth full of bread. Ramose didn't understand it, but he nodded anyway. He walked out of the village. His friend Hapu was waiting for him.

"Where's the scribe?" asked Hapu.

"He's still stuffing his face," said Ramose scornfully. "He's too fat and slow. Let him come at his own speed."

The two boys set off together on the dusty path to the Great Place.

Hapu was an apprentice painter at Pharaoh's tomb. He'd only found out a few weeks before that his friend was actually a prince—he was still getting used to the idea.

The construction of Pharaoh's tomb had been going on for three years. The quarry men had painstakingly chiselled out a long sloping shaft that cut deep into the rock of the valley. At the end of the shaft was a burial chamber and storage rooms where the goods for Pharaoh's afterlife would be stored. Everything Pharaoh needed would be packed into those rooms. There would be furniture, chariots, fine clothing and games. And of course rich and beautiful crowns, collars and armbands, so that he could live in the afterlife as he had in the world. The tomb was nearly finished.

When they reached the tomb, Hapu immediately disappeared into its depths to start work. He was painting the borders of the scenes painted on the tomb walls—which was all an apprentice was permitted to do. Ramose walked over to the store room where he collected an oil lamp and a fresh ink block. Outside the tomb entrance was a pile of stone flakes that the quarry men had chipped from the inside of the tomb. Ramose used the stone flakes to write on, as papyrus was too expensive for these daily tasks. The pile of stone flakes was just one of several piles and was higher than his head. He would never run out of writing materials. Only Paneb's monthly reports to the vizier were written on papyrus. Ramose selected a thin piece of stone about the size of his hand. He would use it for his first task of the day, making a list of all the men who had reported for work.

He lit his lamp, took a deep breath and started to walk down the dark shaft. Ramose didn't like being underground. He felt okay in the shaft, where he could see the square of light which was the tomb entrance. When he had to go into the burial chamber, though, he always felt a wave of panic and imagined that the tons of rock above his head were about to fall in on top of him, burying him alive. He turned round to look back at the tomb entrance. He was all right.

There were other lamps at intervals down the shaft and, about halfway down, there was a larger pool of light. A team of sculptors was carving the walls of the shaft. They were carefully chipping away the soft rock with copper chisels, following the rough drawings sketched on the surface by outliners.

Ramose stopped to write a list of the sculptors' names on his stone flake. He took a reed pen from his pen box. He chewed on the end to make sure that it had a nice soft brush and dipped it in the small container of water that he carried. Then he rubbed the pen onto the new block of black ink which he'd set into his palette. He wrote down the sculptors' names in his untidy handwriting.

"Be careful down there, Ramose," said one of the sculptors. "You never know when the ceiling might collapse and bring the whole mountain down on your head."

The sculptors all laughed. They thought it was very amusing that a tomb worker was afraid of enclosed spaces. Ramose was used to their jokes. He continued on down the tomb shaft.

Next was a group of painters who were bringing the sculptures to life with their bright colours. Ramose noted down their names as well.

At the bottom of the shaft was a chamber with the ceiling covered in yellow stars. Painters were working on the walls, painting prayers asking the gods to help Pharaoh journey safely through the underworld. Ramose turned to look back up the shaft. The square of light that was the tomb entrance looked small enough to fit in his hand. He took another deep breath and turned away from the light and descended the steps to the burial chamber. As quickly as he could, he noted down the tomb workers who were working in there, including Hapu, and then hurried out, back to where he could see the square of daylight again.

Ramose spent the morning checking all the painted texts to make sure that the painters had copied them correctly.

"I think I'll have my meal here in the tomb today," said Paneb at midday.

Paneb avoided walking up and down the tomb shaft as much as possible.

"Bring me down some food, Ramose."

Ramose didn't argue. When he'd first come to work in the tomb the muscles in his legs had been painfully sore. Now he'd walked up and down the steep slope of the tomb shaft so many times that he hardly noticed it. The muscles in his legs had grown strong.

"What's the special occasion?" Ramose asked the cook when he returned from delivering the scribe's food and could finally attend to his own meal. He looked hungrily at the unusually lavish spread of food.

"It's the feast day of Bastet, the cat goddess," said the cook, who used to be a sculptor until he'd lost two fingers when part of a tomb had collapsed. "No one celebrates it down here in the south, but in the Delta where I come from there's a big festival. I like to make something special for the goddess on her day."

Ramose helped himself to the food that was spread out for the workers' midday meal. He heaped freshly cooked lamb, bean stew and boiled eggs into his bowl.

"Pity it's not Bastet's feast day every day," he said. He felt something soft and warm brushing around his legs. A sleek, sandy-coloured creature with eyes the colour of greenstone was wrapping itself around Ramose's legs. It was the cook's cat. It had a gold earring in one delicately pointed ear. On a leather string around its neck was a small ceramic square with a Horus eye painted on it. This was to protect the animal from danger. The cat was miaowing loudly.

"Mery likes lamb," said the cook, smiling at his pampered pet. "She wouldn't mind if you shared a bit with her."

"I like lamb too," said Ramose, thinking that the cook's cat looked well-fed enough.

Hapu was piling a second helping into his own bowl. He couldn't help staring at the way the cook managed to do things with his three-fingered hand.

"What are these?" Ramose asked pointing to a pile of sticky balls on a platter, hoping the man hadn't seen Hapu staring.

"They're fig and nut cakes," the cook replied. "Rolled in honey. And there won't be enough for all the workers if your friend takes so many."

Hapu put two of the sticky balls back on the platter and licked his fingers. He and Ramose walked back to their hut and sat down to eat. The hut was nothing more than a pile of rocks roofed over with a few palm fronds, but it was the boys' home while they were in the Great Place. Ramose picked up one of the large eggs.

"I haven't eaten an ibis egg since I was at—"

Hapu dug him in the ribs. "Samut's over there," he whispered. "Watch what you're saying."

Ramose glanced over his shoulder. The foreman of the tomb was talking to another tomb worker. Ramose was normally more careful. He peeled his egg and bit into it.

"Save one of your cakes for Karoya," Ramose said. "I'd like to take some home for her."

Hapu looked at his friend. "Why should I give my food to her?"

"She probably hasn't tasted anything like them," said Ramose.

The cat came and sat next to Ramose watching very closely as he ate his food. It miaowed again. It wasn't a polite request, it was a demand. Ramose gave it a piece of meat to keep it quiet. The cat ate it delicately.

"Karoya would like a cat like this," he said.

"I've never met anyone so concerned about a slave," grumbled Hapu pushing one of the sweet cakes to the side of his bowl.

"I feel responsible for her. If my father's army hadn't captured her, she'd still be living in freedom with her family in Kush."

"Pharaoh's army has captured thousands of slaves. What difference does it make if one of them is a little happier than the rest?"

"It makes a difference to me," replied Ramose, then he lowered his voice. "When I become pharaoh, the first thing I will do is free her."

"What about the other thousands of slaves?" asked Hapu eating his last fig cake.

Ramose thought for a moment. It would be hard being pharaoh, there would be so many difficult decisions to make.

"I'll free them all," he replied.

"And who will grind the grain?" asked Hapu.

"I'll let the vizier worry about that."

2

FURY OF THE GODS

HAPU FINISHED his food and put his bowl down in the sand. He sighed contentedly and leaned back against the wall of the hut with his hands behind his head. His smile faded slightly.

"The sky's a strange colour."

Ramose looked up at the large oval of sky above the valley. It was darkening. Light grey clouds were drifting over the valley. A breeze suddenly picked up. It was more than a breeze. It was a wind strong enough to blow over one of the water jars. It wasn't the hot wind that occasionally blew from the desert. It was cool. Ramose shivered.

"What's happening?" asked Hapu.

There was a low rumble in the distance. The clouds grew darker as they moved across the valley and covered the sun. As they stared at the sky the boys saw a flash of bright light zigzag from the clouds to the pyramid-shaped peak of the mountain known as the Gate of Heaven. The rumbling noise came again and grew until it exploded in a loud crack.

"The gods must be angry," said Hapu. He was plainly terrified. "They're attacking us."

The sky above the valley was completely covered with black clouds. It was like evening instead of midday. More lightning flashed around the mountain followed immediately by a louder crack of thunder. A large drop of water fell on Ramose's upturned face. Then another. Within a few seconds water was pouring from the sky.

"It's raining," Ramose said, hardly able to believe his eyes.

Hapu stared in amazement as the large drops of water falling from the sky were replaced by even larger lumps of ice. Round ice stones the size of walnuts started pelting down on them.

"Quick," yelled Ramose. "The tomb. We can shelter in the tomb."

The boys ran towards the tomb entrance. Other tomb workers were doing the same. The cook, abandoning his cooking pots, picked up the cat and ran with the boys. They reached the tomb and watched in disbelief as the ice stones continued to fall. The tomb workers shook their heads. The cook's cat was yowling loudly, adding to the eerie feeling that something terrible was about to happen.

"This is a bad omen," said one of the sculptors. "I've heard of rain falling in the desert before, but I've never heard of anything like this."

Ramose remembered when he was younger seeing a heavy shower of rain on a royal visit to the northern city of Memphis. Hapu, who had lived all his life in the south, had never seen rain before. In Egypt people were used to their water coming from the Nile, not from the sky. If the gods were throwing ice stones at them, it was indeed a bad sign.

The ice stones stopped as suddenly as they started and were replaced by rain again, even heavier than before.

"The earth will be covered with water. We'll drown," said Hapu who was almost in tears.

"It'll stop soon," said Ramose, trying to reassure his friend, but he was scared himself.

As if to contradict Ramose's words, there was another rumbling noise. This time it didn't come from the sky but from the ground. It didn't fade or end in a crack, it grew. It was coming from the direction of the Gate of Heaven, the cobra goddess's mountain home.

Ramose watched the familiar slopes of the mountain turn to liquid mud as water foamed down them. Then a wave of water appeared over the edge of the high desert on the western side of the mountain and rushed down its slopes in a foamy surge. The ground beneath their feet began to shake. The noise of the advancing water turned from a rumble to a roar as water continued to pour from the high desert down the mountain slopes. As the size of the wave grew, so did the noise.

It was like nothing Ramose had ever heard before, deafening and frightening. A wall of water crashed down the lower slopes and began to surge across the valley floor. The water was brown with mud. Stones and rocks were carried along in the flow, gouging a deep rut in the sand. Boulders the size of houses were washed down from the slopes of the mountain as if they were pebbles. The wall of water was rushing across the valley at such a speed that Ramose and the other tomb workers stood and stared at it in disbelief.

As it got closer the wave grew bigger. Ramose

calculated that it must be at least ten cubits high. The cook's cat yowled again and struggled out of her master's arms and darted out of the tomb. Ramose suddenly realised that the terrible wave was heading straight for them.

"We have to get to higher ground," Ramose yelled, "or we'll be washed away."

The tomb makers suddenly leapt to life and ran out of the tomb entrance. They didn't have time to get across the valley to the path that led to the village. Instead they followed the cat which was clambering up the cliffs around the tomb entrance. Hapu didn't move, he was mesmerised by the awful brown wave.

"Hapu, come on!" shouted Ramose, but the roar of the approaching water drowned his feeble voice.

Ramose grabbed his friend's arm and pulled him along. Hapu finally tore his eyes away from the water and started scrambling up the cliff. The rain battered down on them. Rivulets of water pouring down the cliff loosened stones, making it hard for them to climb. Every time they grabbed a stone for a handhold it would slip out of its muddy hole and fall to the valley floor.

Ramose turned to look for Hapu who was struggling below him. The wall of brown water was coursing across the valley. The storehouse and the workers' makeshift huts were smashed by the crest of the wave. The place where minutes before they had sat in the sun eating their meal disappeared beneath the surging water.

The wave would be on them in a few seconds. Ramose looked for a way up the sheer cliff face. Water was sluicing down it like a waterfall. Other men were trying to climb up the cliff, but it was too steep and slippery with rain. He saw someone slip and fall. He knew that if he didn't think of something quickly he and his friend would face the same fate.

The familiar dirty-yellow colour of the cliff had turned brown in the rain. Ramose saw a darker brown stripe in the rock face to his left. It was a crevice, a vertical split in the cliff. Hapu's hands were groping wildly around Ramose's feet. Ramose reached down, grabbed his friend's arm and yanked him up. He shouted at him, telling him to shelter in the crevice. His words were completely swallowed by the roar of the water. Hapu was blinking the rain out of his eyes, too frightened and stunned to comprehend what Ramose was trying to do.

Ramose pushed Hapu into the crevice, but didn't have time to squeeze in himself. The wave of water hit the cliff with a crushing force. Ramose glimpsed other workers washed from the cliff as the side of his head crashed against the rock. Gritty water filled his mouth and nose. He couldn't move. The weight of the water pushed him against the rock. I'm going to die, he thought, squashed like an insect under god's thumb.

The wave split into two streams around the cliff face and Ramose felt himself being ripped off the cliff face by one of the streams and washed along in its furious course. The tumbling water tossed him like a reed. There was water all around him. He couldn't tell which way the surface was. He tried to scream out in terror, but only got a mouthful of muddy water.

Ramose felt the grasping hands of drowning men grab at his arms and legs. Now he knew which way was down. I don't want to die, he thought. He kicked out to stop them dragging him down with them. His lungs were ready to burst. He opened his eyes. He could see nothing but murky brown water. He kicked again and his head broke the surface.

He gulped in air, but still couldn't see through the sand and silt that filled his eyes. He reached out blindly. His hand banged against stone as the stream dragged him along and his fingers struck a protruding rock. He grabbed at it with both hands and heaved himself up onto it. The rushing water pulled at him, but he clung to the rock gasping for air. He felt sharp points stick into his back and then something climbing up his back and onto his shoulder.

By the time Ramose had blinked the sand out
of his eyes the rain had stopped. The water still
rushed past, but it was losing its force. There
was a forlorn yowling in his ear. He reached up
to his shoulder. There was something clinging
there, covered with wet fur. It was the cook's cat,
terrified but still alive. Ramose straddled the rock
with the wet cat in his arms. A feeling of elation
burst inside him, he wanted to shout out loud.
He was alive, he'd cheated death. The gods had
poured down their fury and he had survived.

The water was disappearing, oozing through
cracks and ravines, soaking into the sand. The
sky was a strange orange colour as the sun fought
to break through the thinning clouds. It cast an
unearthly light on the Great Place. The rocks
shone. The valley was an unfamiliar place. The
rushing waters had completely resculpted the
valley floor with wet sand and huge boulders.
The remains of the huts and the storehouse
were buried under two cubits of brown mud. A
deep ravine had been cut down the middle of the
valley where the main force of the flood had bored
along.

Ramose realised that he was naked. The flood
waters had ripped his kilt from him. He could
taste the metallic taste of blood in the water that
dripped from his hair. Blood was seeping from
cuts and grazes all over his body. He stood up

shakily and looked around. Others emerged from the shelter of the rocks. Ramose clambered stiffly down the rock, dizzy with the joy of being alive. He waded through the knee-deep sludge that was now the new valley floor, still holding on to the cat.

The mud sucked at Ramose's legs as he made his way towards the tomb entrance. He couldn't find it. It wasn't there any more. The cliff above it had collapsed and fallen into the mud.

The mud around him grew too deep to wade through. There was a soft moist noise like a contented belch after a good meal. The bog around him shifted slightly and a body floated to the surface. The face was bruised and battered beyond recognition, but one hand had two fingers missing. Ramose's joy, turned to horror and then to fear. He was alive, but others had died. What about Hapu? He prayed to Amun, king of the gods, that his friend was still alive.

The clouds moved away to the south and the sun appeared again. The surviving tomb makers slowly made their way to higher ground and gathered together in a dazed and bruised group. Ramose looked frantically at their faces. Hapu wasn't among them. He clambered back down to where he had left his friend. That section of the cliff was still standing. Hapu was still wedged in the crevice where Ramose had pushed him.

He gently pulled his friend out. His face was covered in deep gashes, his nose was pushed to one side, his lip was split and pouring blood. His eyelids flickered as Ramose pulled him out into the sunlight. He was still alive, but unconscious. Ramose's face which had just dried in the sun, was wet again. This time with tears of relief. With the cat clinging to his shoulder, Ramose carried Hapu back to where the stunned survivors were huddled together.

A group of women and children from the village appeared on the rim of the valley. They had heard the terrible roar of the water from the village. Ianna, the scribe's wife, was among them, so was Karoya.

"Are you all right?" she said taking the striped cloth that she wore over her head and giving it to Ramose with her head turned away.

Ramose had forgotten that he was naked. He quickly wrapped the cloth around himself.

"Yes, I'm okay, but I'm not sure about Hapu." Ramose gently wiped the mud and blood from his friend's face.

Ianna was looking frantically from face to face.

"Where is Paneb?" she asked in a quavery voice.

Ramose hadn't given the scribe a thought. He had been down in the tomb when the storm hit. The scribe was fat and slow. He would have heard the roar of the approaching water, but would never have made it up the shaft in time. Ianna let out a wail that echoed around the valley. Other women who had been unable to find their husbands and fathers joined in. The eerie wailing gave Ramose goose skin, despite the fact that the sun had already dried and warmed him.

"What's that?" asked Karoya pointing to the damp, furry bulge in the crook of Ramose's arm.

"It's for you," he said and held out the cat to her.

3

AFTERMATH

THE STORM had lasted for only half an hour, but it had changed the lives of the tomb workers forever. Of the eighteen men who worked in Pharaoh's tomb, only six had survived the flood. Ten women had lost their husbands. Twenty-three children were fatherless. Hapu, whose mother had died the previous year, was orphaned. Pharaoh's tomb was ruined.

The heavy rain had damaged the village, mud bricks had melted away in the downpour, cellars had been flooded, but the damage was soon repaired. Hapu, though stunned, cut and bruised, was soon recovering.

Ianna wandered from room to room in the house, not knowing what to do with herself. "His soul will be lost," she cried. "He will never find peace."

Ramose hadn't liked the scribe much, but he would never have wished this on him. His body was buried under the great weight of stones and sand that the flood had washed into Pharaoh's tomb. There would be no mummy to place in the hillside tomb that Paneb had been preparing, at great expense, for his own burial.

"The sculptors will make a statue of Paneb to place in his tomb." Ramose had tried to console her. "His spirit will live in the statue. He will find peace."

Five days after the flood, Vizier Wersu stood in the valley of the Great Place on a pile of sand and rocks. The royal architect, a man called Ineni, was explaining the situation to him.

"The tomb entrance under us is buried beneath several cubits of sand and rocks. The sculptured walls will be cracked, scored and broken. The tomb itself will certainly be full of water. The burial chamber may have collapsed."

Ramose was standing at a respectful distance with the other surviving tomb workers trying to catch the architect's words.

"While the rocks and sand could eventually be removed," Ineni told them, "it would take years, decades, perhaps even a century, for the water to seep away."

The vizier said nothing. His thin mouth was grim. His bony insect hands were clasped behind his back.

"It is my recommendation, Vizier," continued the architect, "that a new tomb should be excavated with the entrance on higher ground." He said it as casually as if he was talking about weaving a new basket or making a stool.

There was a murmur among the tomb workers. They had all been working on Pharaoh's tomb for three years.

The vizier turned to the workers. Ramose kept to the back of the group. His face was cut and bruised and he didn't think the vizier would recognise him, but he didn't want to take the risk. Ramose avoided Wersu's evil eyes.

"I agree with Architect Ineni," said the vizier. "A new tomb must be commenced." He looked around at the battered and bruised team of workers as if he was bored with the situation. "There is another matter which is of importance to this project." He paused while he adjusted the folds of his robes.

"Pharaoh has fallen ill in Memphis. He is very ill. It is feared that he may be rested from life before the year's end."

Ramose stared at the vizier's dispassionate face. He might have been telling them that there was no beer for their midday meal or that the cost of chisels had increased.

For Ramose the news was staggering. His father was dying. When he died, Ramose would be the rightful heir to the kingship, but since everyone thought he was dead the crown would go to his half-brother, the horrible brat Tuthmosis.

"So then, work must start on the new tomb immediately," said the vizier.

The tomb workers turned to go back to the village. They knew they had a huge task in front of them, but they were Pharaoh's tomb builders and they were willing to do whatever they had to in order to finish his tomb in time.

"There is one more thing." The vizier's voice was thick with what sounded like pleasure.

The workers turned back.

"Pharaoh's new tomb is to be built with the entrance higher in the cliff face. It will be a difficult excavation. Time is short. You are now few."

He looked around at the six remaining tomb workers and the two apprentices. "I will send for the gangs of temple craftsmen working in Thebes and in Memphis. They will take charge of the work. You will be sent to work somewhere else."

The tomb workers stood in stunned silence for a moment as Vizier Wersu walked away and climbed into a covered chair. Four porters lifted the chair and carried the vizier away towards the city. The tomb workers all started shouting at once.

"They can't send us away."

"We are Pharaoh's tomb makers."

"This is our home!"

"Where will we be sent?" Ramose asked the architect.

"You have been appointed to Tombos," replied the architect. There was a shiver of exclamations through the small group. "You will have the honour of working on a fortress and temple commemorating Pharaoh's great victories over Egypt's enemies."

Ramose walked back to the tomb makers' village on legs that felt like they were made out of soft mud. He kept his distance from the other workers. He needed time to get used to these new circumstances. Only a week ago he'd thought of his life in the village as a tedious chore. He thought he would have done anything to get out of it. Now that it was suddenly all about to change, he found himself wishing it wasn't over.

He went back to the scribe's house. Ianna

was lying on a couch, weeping. Hapu came in and slowly lowered himself onto a stool. He was still weak and hadn't been to the meeting with Wersu.

"I've just walked around the garden," he said sounding exhausted.

Now that he had no family of his own, Hapu had been recovering in the scribe's house where Karoya could look after him. His injuries were worse than Ramose's. His face was still swollen and bruised, his broken nose permanently squashed sideways. His whole body was stiff and sore. Karoya came in with wine for her grieving mistress, beer for Ramose and a thick brown potion for her patient. The cat, Mery, followed closely at her heels.

Hapu pulled a face as he sipped at the potion. "I'm sure you're trying to poison me," he said to Karoya.

"It is a remedy from Kush, made from burnt lotus leaves and the fruit of the castor oil plant. It will help heal your body."

Hapu drank it down in one gulp. "What did the vizier say?" he asked.

"A new tomb is to be built," replied Ramose quietly.

Hapu nodded. It was what they had expected.

"And excavation has to start immediately," continued Ramose blankly. He was still numb with shock. "Pharaoh is dying."

Hapu and Karoya both turned to Ramose. They knew what this meant to him.

"May Osiris protect him," muttered Hapu.

"That's not the only thing," said Ramose. "New gangs will build the tomb. We will be sent to Tombos."

Hapu looked at Ramose in disbelief. "Tombos? Where's Tombos?" he asked. "I've never heard of this place."

Ramose had heard of it. He knew all the details of his father's campaigns. it was a small town only recently conquered by Pharaoh's army.

"It's a town at the very southern edge of Egypt, beyond the third cataract."

Hapu was stunned. "I've never been south of the city. I've never been north of it either. I've spent my whole life in Thebes. I thought I'd grow old here."

Hapu knew that the Nile, in its journey from its source deep in foreign lands, was not the silent, slow-moving river that they were familiar with. It was a noisy, foaming stream that cascaded over a series of rocky outcrops. These were known as the cataracts. Until Pharaoh's recent conquest, the first cataract had marked the edge of Egypt.

"I don't want to live beyond the third cataract," said Hapu. "That's in the lands of the barbarian sand-dwellers."

Karoya looked annoyed. "Why do Egyptians

think everyone outside their land is a barbarian? I should like to go to this place. It will be closer to my home."

"He doesn't mean to offend you, Karoya," Ramose said. "No one likes to leave their homeland."

The tomb makers and their families left the village after the funerals. Only two of the missing bodies had been found. They had been sent to Thebes for mummification. All the other men had had statues made for their tombs. This meant that they didn't have to wait the usual seventy days until the mummification process was complete. Now that they were used to the idea, the villagers seemed anxious to leave. Their few possessions were piled on a sled which the men took it in turns to pull.

Ramose could easily carry his possessions. He had slightly less than he'd had when he arrived at the village. Since he lost his kilt in the flood, he didn't even have a change of clothing. He still had the gold, melted down into thick rings, that Keneben had given him. He had the scribal tools that he'd used in the schoolroom back at the palace, but which had been too rich and ornate for him to use in the village without attracting attention. He also had his heart scarab hidden at the bottom of his bag. This was the large beetle-shaped jewel that was to be buried with him when he died. Hapu had taken a stool and a chest that his father had made. Karoya, the slave girl, had more baggage than either of them. She had a large bag which contained her favourite cooking pot and the round stone that she used for grinding grain. She was also carrying a basket made of woven rushes under her arm. The basket had an open grille woven into the lid to let air in.

"You shouldn't have brought that, Karoya," grumbled Hapu, who was now recovered enough to walk to Thebes. "Slaves aren't supposed to have possessions. You should be helping me carry my things."

"Carry your own baggage," Karoya snapped.

Ramose smiled as he listened to his friends bicker. He knew Hapu would never get the better of Karoya. Through the lid of Karoya's rush basket, Hapu could see two glinting green eyes. She was carrying the cat that Ramose had saved from the flood.

"Mery is mine," said Karoya firmly. "She comes with me."

The ragged group straggled up the path that led from the tomb makers' village to the city. They reached the top of the hill and the blue strip of the Nile was suddenly visible in the distance with a band of green vegetation on either side. The temples and the city were on the other side

of the river. On this side was the palace, its whitewashed walls dazzling in the sun, its gold-tipped
flagpoles glinting. Ramose turned to look back
at the village. From that height its mud brick
walls seemed to merge with the valley floor. It
was a strange place for a prince to have spent six
months of his life. He was glad to be leaving the
miserable little village, but, on the other hand, he
wasn't sorry he had experienced living there.

"Come on, Ramose," Hapu called out. "You're
getting left behind."

In less than half an hour Ramose was back
in the familiar fertile Nile Valley that he hadn't
seen for eight months. The landscape changed
suddenly from dry, dusty desert to green fields
and orchards. Ramose breathed in deeply.

"Smell that," he said to his friends. "Isn't it
wonderful?"

The air was laden with the fragrance of
pomegranates and slightly fermenting grapes.
Karoya wrinkled her nose. She was a desert-
dweller and the fertile smells of the river valley
were strange to her.

"It smells sort of greenish," she said. "And the
air is heavy."

They passed by the palace walls. Ramose
looked up at the fluttering pennants and the high
windows. Karoya and Hapu exchanged a glance.
Ramose pictured its luxurious interiors: the

massive halls and columns; the comfortable bed with the thick linen mattress; his own room with the wall paintings of Amun, king of the gods, and of his father hunting in the Delta. He wondered if his sister, Hatshepsut, was in the palace. More than likely she had travelled up to Memphis to be with their father. There was nothing for him at the palace now. His nanny was dead, his tutor sent abroad. He would be a stranger in his own home.

They reached the edge of the river and the foreman herded them onto a ferry made of bundles of papyrus reeds lashed together. Karoya was very anxious about getting onto the boat.

"We're just going across the river," said Ramose, trying to encourage her. "It's quite safe."

"I don't like the river," she said flatly. "Too much water is bad."

After his experience in the flood, Ramose could not argue with her. He helped her aboard and found her somewhere to sit, away from the sides of the boat. Mery was miaowing plaintively from her basket. It sounded like she shared her mistress's dislike of the river.

Ramose was happy to be on the river. He trailed his hand in its cool blue waters and felt the fresh breeze on his face.

They spent the night on the roof of Ianna's brother's house in the noisy, sprawling city.

Ianna was going to stay in Thebes and live with her brother. Karoya was to stay and serve her. Ramose and Hapu would be apprenticed to new workers in Tombos. The two boys were to leave the following morning, sailing south with the rest of the workers from the Great Place.

Ramose woke before daybreak and got up. He picked up his bag and quietly crept across the roof to the stairs. He looked back to check that he hadn't disturbed his friends and tripped over something soft and furry. Ramose crashed to the floor and Mery screeched with pain. Karoya and Hapu sat upright at the same time.

"What's going on?" said Hapu sleepily.

Karoya was wide awake immediately. "Where do you think you're going?" she said.

The sky was starting to lighten to the east and she could make out Ramose sprawled on the floor. He was wearing his cloak and his bag was slung over his shoulder. Mery jumped onto Karoya's lap and looked at Ramose as reproachfully as her mistress.

"I think that cat tripped me up on purpose," said Ramose getting to his feet.

"Of course she did," said Karoya. "She knew that you shouldn't be sneaking off in the night by yourself."

Ramose looked at the pink glow in the sky. "It isn't the night."

"What are you doing up so early?" asked Hapu rubbing his eyes. "The boat to Tombos doesn't leave till mid-morning."

"I'm not going to Tombos," said Ramose. "I'm going to Memphis to see my father."

4

RIVER JOURNEY

"AND YOU weren't even going to say goodbye?" Karoya was sitting with her arms folded crossly.

"I thought it would be better if you were as surprised as everyone else. I didn't want you to get into trouble."

"I'm coming with you," said Hapu, scrambling to his feet.

"I have to hurry," said Ramose gathering up his things. "The boat to Memphis leaves soon."

"I suppose once you're pharaoh you won't be interested in having an apprentice painter for a friend."

"Certainly not a slave."

"That's not true. I was just concerned about your safety. It'll be dangerous when I get to Memphis. I have enemies there. My father is ill. It won't be easy to get to see him."

His friends sat in silence.

"I'll send for both of you when it's safe. I promise."

"If it's going to be so difficult, you'll need help," said Hapu rolling up his reed mat. "And anything's better than going to Tombos."

Ramose didn't have time to argue. He couldn't decide whether he was glad or not that his friends were coming with him. He appreciated the company, but three people wandering around Egypt were a lot more obvious than one. They had to work out a story.

It was easy enough to get on the boat to Memphis. The boatman was happy to carry them without asking questions once he had one of Ramose's gold rings in his hand.

It was a long way to Memphis. The winds blew from the north, any boat sailing south only had to put up a sail to be carried down the Nile.

Travelling north wasn't so easy and the wooden boat had a crew of oarsmen to push it against the prevailing wind. They were away before most people were awake.

The journey was going to take two weeks at least. Ramose would have plenty of time to think about what he would do when he arrived in the northern city. The boatman was very curious about his young passengers. Ramose told him the story that they had invented—that he and Hapu had been apprenticed to workers at the temple of Ptah. He pulled out a scroll of papyrus and showed the boatman. The boatman looked at the squiggly writing and the important-looking red seal on the bottom and nodded.

"The old temple is being rebuilt," said Ramose. Hapu nodded knowledgeably. "The slave girl will cook for us on our journey." Karoya tried to look like an obedient servant.

The boatman looked suspiciously at Mery, who was miaowing loudly and unhappily from her basket.

"A present for the lady of the household where we will be staying," explained Ramose. Hapu nodded again.

The boatman seemed satisfied with their story and went off to shout at the oarsmen.

Hapu waited until he was well out of earshot before he spoke. "That papyrus is the list of food sent to the Great Place from the city last month!"

Ramose grinned. "I knew he wouldn't be able to read."

"So I am your slave as usual," said Karoya.

"You *are* a slave, Karoya," said Hapu. "What else was he supposed to say?"

"He could have said I was a princess from Kush going to pay tribute to Pharaoh."

"I don't think you're quite dressed for the part. And where are all your servants, Your Highness?"

"Stop arguing, you two," said Ramose. "The boatman will hear."

He glanced over at the boatman who was now settling down for a rest.

"You will have to be our slave while we are travelling, Karoya. Anything else would just attract attention. I promise you that as soon as I am pharaoh, the first thing I will do is grant you freedom and see that you are returned to your homeland."

They were the only passengers on the boat. The boat had a cargo of logs, precious hardwood from the southern lands. After they had been travelling for two days, Karoya let Mery out of her basket. The cat sniffed around the boat suspiciously, but soon got used to the idea of living on a boat. Karoya was still uncomfortable with so much water around her. She sat in the middle of the boat with her eyes fixed firmly on the shore.

Ramose and Hapu fished and played senet. They watched the land slip by them on either side. They saw brief scenes from people's lives as they passed: women pounding dirty clothes with rocks, a man trying to move a stubborn ox, a child crying over a lost ball that was floating out of reach.

Each evening the boat was moored and Karoya went off in search of dry reeds and animal dung to make a cooking fire. They ate a simple meal of bread and fish, and then slept on the boat on their reed mats. When they stopped at a town they bought more food. Ramose had exchanged two of his gold rings for copper. It attracted too much attention when they offered gold in exchange for flour and vegetables.

The journey was taking longer than Ramose had expected. After a week on board the boat, they had only reached Akhmim, which by Ramose's reckoning was only a third of the way to Memphis. At this rate it was going to take a lot of gold to keep the three of them fed on the journey. Actually there were four mouths to feed as Mery had to have a daily supply of fish and milk.

"Look," whispered Hapu as if he had read Ramose's thoughts. "Over there."

Ramose looked over to where Hapu was pointing. A rat was walking calmly along the edge of the boat. It hopped from there onto one of the logs strapped to the deck. Mery was curled up asleep in her open basket totally unaware of the rat.

"Did you see that?" said Hapu to Karoya. "There was a rat. That cat of yours didn't even notice it! It's useless. All it does is eat our food, drink our milk and make that awful wailing noise when we're trying to sleep."

"Sounds a bit like you," said Karoya scratching Mery behind the ear.

"I don't wail," said Hapu.

Ramose ignored his friends' bickering and returned to his thoughts. He knew he'd need gold to bribe people once he got to the palace if he was going to get anywhere near his father. He wondered if his supply of gold was enough.

"I'm bored," said Hapu. "How much further is it?"

Ramose was beginning to wish that he'd managed to sneak away on his own. Hapu and Karoya were either complaining about being on a boat for so long or arguing with each other.

"Nobody asked you to come," said Ramose irritably. "But just remember that if you weren't on this boat, Hapu, you'd be on another one heading for alien lands beyond the reaches of Egypt. And you, Karoya, would be Ianna's slave."

His friends didn't say anything. Ramose had to admit he was sick of the boat as well. It wasn't like the royal barge that had taken him up and down the river when he was still a prince. Then he'd had a comfortable bed, servants to attend to his slightest need, and as much food as he wished to eat.

Later that evening they were sitting on board the boat eating their evening meal.

"Can't we get some meat?" Hapu grumbled. "I'm sick of fish." He was just about to put a piece of fish in his mouth when Mery strode up importantly and dropped something in his lap. Hapu looked down. It was a dead rat. He leapt to his feet with a yell.

"You said you wanted meat!" said Karoya.

It was the first time Ramose had laughed in quite a while.

Another six days brought them to a town called Hardai. The royal barge had never stopped there. Ramose didn't like the look of it. It was just a collection of mud brick houses and dusty streets.

The people didn't smile, they were not friendly. Karoya got into an argument with a woman who was trying to sell her some rotten grapes when she wanted figs. The three friends walked back towards the boat and for once they were pleased to be getting back on board. The boatman was sitting on the wharf waiting for them. He looked up and grinned as they approached.

"It's going to cost you another twenty deben of copper to go all the way to Memphis," he said while picking at a scab on his hand.

Ramose looked at him in disbelief. "What are you talking about? We already paid you for the whole trip."

"The winds have been stronger than expected," said the boatman. "It's taking longer than I thought."

"What difference does that make?" shouted Hapu angrily. "We aren't eating your food."

"The extra weight is slowing us down."

"That's nonsense," said Ramose. "We weigh nothing compared to your cargo."

He jerked his head towards the huge logs on board the boat.

"And Mery has caught three rats since we've been on your dirty boat," added Karoya.

"An extra twenty deben or you stay here," said the boatman.

Ramose was furious. "Okay we stay here."

The boatman called his bluff. "I'm casting off."

"Go then," said Ramose stubbornly. "We'll find another boat going to Memphis."

"Hardai's not the place to spend the night outdoors," said the man, unwinding the rope that tied up his boat.

"Ramose," whispered Hapu. "There might not be another boat for days."

Ramose was too angry to listen to reason.

The boatman threw the rope on board. He jumped aboard himself.

"This is your last chance," he said.

Ramose said nothing.

"Row!" shouted the boatman to his oarsmen.

The boat moved away from the quay leaving the three companions stranded in Hardai.

5

AN ANCIENT SCROLL

"**I** DON'T THINK that was a good idea," said Hapu as he watched the boat shrink into the distance.

The only other boats at the quay were local fishing boats made of papyrus reeds.

"Now what are we going to do?" moaned Hapu.

"We'll have to spend the night here," replied Ramose. "You were both desperate to get off that boat. Now we are off it, and you are still complaining."

"There's nowhere I can make a fire," said Karoya. "The streets are crowded and there's no open land. We'll have to walk into the countryside."

"I don't like the idea of that," said Ramose, looking at the unfriendly people. "We'll have to see if someone will sell us a cooked meal and maybe let us sleep on their roof.

Everywhere they asked, people wanted many deben of copper to let the travellers share their meagre meal and sleep on their roof. They stood in the dirty main street of the town. They were all starting to wish they were back on board the cargo boat.

"You don't want to stay in this place," said a voice at Ramose's shoulder. It was a short man with a beard and eyes that looked in different directions. "It's full of thieves."

"We don't have much choice," Ramose said. "There are no other boats leaving for the north."

"I'm aboard a naval boat, taking men up to the Delta," the man replied. "I could talk to the captain for you. I'm sure he wouldn't mind if you sailed with us. We've just stopped to buy some fresh meat. We'll be leaving again in about an hour."

The three friends returned to the wharf. While they had been searching the town for somewhere to spend the night, the naval boat had tied up. It was a sleek craft. Ramose grinned at Hapu and Karoya as they boarded the boat. They couldn't believe their luck.

"This is more like it," said Hapu as they moved off.

The naval boat was bigger, cleaner and faster. It cut through the water at twice the speed of the cargo boat under the power of twenty soldiers at the oars. The captain stood at the stern shouting orders and operating the rudder oar.

They travelled until it was dark and then camped on the riverbank. Their camping place was away from any town or village and it was very peaceful. The soldiers invited them to share their food.

After they'd eaten all the lamb and onions they could, they laid out their reed mats on the sandy shore beneath a grove of date palms.

"It's good to be away from that awful town," said Karoya looking up at the stars through the palm fronds.

"Maybe our luck's changed," said Hapu.

Ramose listened to the stillness of the night and hoped he was right.

Their new friend was called Hori. He was travelling with two other men. One was a big man called Intef, who seemed to have an excess of muscles, but a shortage of brains. The other was called Seth. He had a mean mouth and a scar on his neck as if someone had unsuccessfully tried to chop off his head.

"We're going to Memphis to join the navy," Hori told them over breakfast. "The captain is my sister's husband's brother."

Ramose couldn't help wondering if a man who was cross-eyed would make a good soldier, but he kept his thoughts to himself.

"We're joining a unit that is going to sail over the Great Green to conquer the eastern lands."

Karoya was horrified at the thought of sailing on the sea.

"I've heard that sometimes the boat goes so far out to sea that you can't see the shore." Karoya's eyes were wide. "That can't be true, can it?" she asked.

"It's true," said Hori. "And sometimes the waves rise up to the height of three men."

"Why are you going to do this?" said Karoya. "Why don't you stay on land where it's safe?"

"We were working in the alabaster quarries in the south. It's hard work. I heard that Pharaoh, may he have long life and health, was recruiting for the navy. My friends and I thought we'd give it a try."

Ramose couldn't quite put his finger on it, but there was something he didn't like about Hori and his friends. Perhaps it was the way one of Hori's eyes always seemed to be on him.

They made good progress. "At this rate we'll be in Memphis in two days," said Hapu the next day.

Hapu had been in a very cheerful mood ever since they'd come on board. He chatted happily to Hori, telling them all about the work on Pharaoh's tomb.

"It's supposed to be a secret, Hapu," said Ramose wishing his friend was grumpy and silent again, instead of happy and talkative.

"I haven't said where the tomb is," said Hapu. "And anyway it's destroyed now."

Ramose was starting to get nervous about arriving in Memphis. He had begun to think that he would never regain his place as heir to Egypt's throne, never see his father, never become pharaoh. Suddenly, in two days, he would be able to contact his sister again and see his sick father.

Now that the wait was over, the thought of arriving in Memphis quite scared him. His plan for actually getting inside the palace there was rather vague. He decided that the best thing to do was to find his sister first, but how he would get to her without the vizier knowing he hadn't yet worked out.

Hori came and sat beside him.

"You are a scribe, I see," said Hori looking with one eye at the palette and pen box in Ramose's bag.

"An apprentice scribe," said Ramose.

"That's a nice set of scribal tools," said Hori.

"I inherited it from my previous master, who died in the flood," lied Ramose closing his bag. He was conscious that the ebony palette inlaid with gold, ivory and turquoise was far too rich for an apprentice scribe to own.

"Tell me what you make of this," Hori said pulling a very old-looking piece of papyrus from his own bag.

Ramose noticed that it had a royal seal, though the blob of wax was cracking with age. He unrolled the papyrus and read the flowing script.

"It's instructions," he said.

"Instructions on how to get inside a pyramid?" asked Intef.

Seth thumped him in the chest to silence him.

"No," replied Ramose. "Instructions on how to lead a good life and attain knowledge. I've read many texts like this. My tutor made me copy them out endlessly."

He turned over the scroll. "There is mention of a pyramid, the pyramid of one of the old pharaohs."

The three men leaned forward. "Does it say anything about the tomb within the pyramid?"

"It could be about the location of a tomb, but it's written like a puzzle, a riddle, as if the person who wrote it didn't really want anyone to find it. Where did you get it from?"

"Oh, I just picked it up somewhere," Hori said vaguely. Intef and Seth, who had hardly spoken since they'd been aboard, started whispering to each other. "I'll hand it in to the authorities when we get to Memphis."

They tied up in the afternoon. "Why are we stopping so early?" asked Hapu. "We usually keep going till sunset."

"This is a good place to moor for the night," said the captain. "Further up, the river bank is rocky and it's more difficult to get ashore."

The soldiers set up their camp on shore near some pretty farming land. Some of them used the extra daylight hours to wash their kilts at the river's edge. Others fished with their spears. Karoya helped the cook collect fuel for the cooking fire.

Hapu leaned back comfortably on a ridge of sand. "I shall almost miss this life."

"Make the most of it, you could be in prison this time tomorrow," said Ramose in a low voice. "Arrested for breaking into the palace."

"Don't be so gloomy. It's too nice a day."

The sun was setting and the sky turned pale orange. It was a nice day, but Ramose couldn't help but worry about what might be ahead of them.

They had a pleasant meal of ox meat, newly baked bread and vegetables. After dinner the soldiers played senet and a rather childish ball game. Hapu joined in enthusiastically.

Ramose laid out his reed mat away from the soldiers where it was quieter. The others eventually settled down to sleep, but Ramose lay awake looking at the stars. He couldn't sleep. Hapu was snoring softly. Karoya was sleeping under her head shawl. All the soldiers were asleep as well. The only other creature awake was Mery who was trying to settle down on Ramose's stomach. Ramose had pushed the cat away at least half a dozen times, but it kept coming back, digging its claws into his chest. Ramose sat up abruptly and grabbed the cat. He stuffed it into his reed bag.

"Now perhaps you'll go to sleep and leave me alone," hissed Ramose.

He tied a leather thong around the opening. The bag was loosely woven, the cat would be able to breathe easily enough. He lay down again with a sigh.

Just as Ramose was starting to drift off to sleep, he felt a hand clamp over his mouth. It was a dirty, sweaty hand that smelt of onions. Ramose tried to pull it off, but other hands turned him over roughly and tied his arms behind his back. A gag was tied tightly over his mouth. Ramose fought furiously against his bindings but he couldn't break free. A short, dark figure hauled him to his feet and forced him to walk away from his friends and into the darkness. He struggled against his captors. They muttered and cursed him. Something cracked him on the head.

6

KIDNAPPED

SOMEONE was slapping his face. It hurt. His whole head hurt. "Come on, wake up," said a rough voice. It was Hori. "Intef's tired of carrying you."

Ramose was lying on the ground. Hori was leaning over him. He slapped him again. Ramose tried to sit up, but he couldn't because his hands were tied behind him. His jaw was stiff and sore.

His mouth was dry because of the tight gag. He rolled onto his side. Ramose didn't know where he was. It was still dark. He couldn't hear the sound of the river, but the air was still moist and he could feel grass beneath him. Hori and Intef were watching him. Seth was opening Ramose's bag. He undid the string. There was a ferocious spitting and hissing as Mery leapt out of the bag. Seth shrieked. Mery darted off into the darkness.

"It's a monster," Seth yelled. "The boy's got a monster in his bag."

Ramose would have laughed if he hadn't had a strip of linen gagging him. He hoped the cat could find its way back to Karoya.

"It was the slave girl's cat, stupid," said Hori. "Let's get moving. We've got a long way to go before it gets light."

Ramose's moment of pleasure disappeared as Intef dragged him to his feet. After walking for about two hours in the dark, the moon rose. Ramose could see two pyramids in the distance, their limestone faces gave off a soft glow in the moonlight. They were walking towards the larger pyramid. It was surrounded by tombs, chapels and temples. As they got closer, Ramose could see that there was a row of trees planted around the edge of the pyramid. There were not only date palms and tamarisks, but also sacred persea trees.

It was starting to get light by now. Ramose was tired. He could tell the other men were as well, but Hori was making them hurry. He led them to a crumbling rectangular tomb where he broke open the door and they went inside just as the sun rose. Inside was a chapel with painted walls. Ramose knew that somewhere below them an important person would be buried.

"No one goes outside until it's dark again," said Hori laying down his reed mat.

"I don't like the idea of sleeping in a tomb," said Seth looking nervously in all the dark corners.

Intef's brow furrowed. "What if I want to…"

"Go now," said Hori. "Seth, you go out and find a temple that's still in use and steal some of the food offerings."

"Do I have to?"

"Yes."

Seth left reluctantly. He soon returned with food and the robbers feasted on the meat, vegetables and sweet cakes that he had stolen from a temple. When they had finished eating, Hori belched loudly.

"Untie the scribe's hands." He nodded to Seth who went over and untied the rope around Ramose's wrists.

They gave him a piece of dry bread and a few mouthfuls of warm beer.

"Intef, you sleep in front of the door," Hori said

as he settled himself down. "Just in case the scribe decides to wander off." He grinned at Seth. "Or in case any spirits try and get us."

They were all asleep within a few minutes. All except for Ramose. He couldn't sleep. Seth had insisted on leaving a lamp burning. In the dim light, Ramose looked at the paintings on the walls of the chapel. He peered at the writing. It was the tomb of a priest called Amenhotep. There was a painting of the priest and his wife, ploughing in the Field of Reeds in the afterlife. Another painting showed the couple praising Osiris. The third wall had a scene from Amenhotep's funeral. The fourth wall showed a banquet with girls dancing and playing musical instruments. In the dim light it reminded Ramose of the palace and his own room with its wall paintings. There was an offering table, but it looked like it had been a very long time since anyone had brought offerings for Amenhotep.

Ramose felt like he'd only just got to sleep when Seth was shaking him awake again.

"Come on, Scribe," he said. "You've got work to do."

Breakfast was another mouthful of dry bread, and three dates. Ramose suspected it was nowhere near breakfast time.

"I'm thirsty."

Hori gave him a flask of beer.

"Don't you have any water?" Ramose asked.

"No."

Outside it was a still, cool evening. It was peaceful. Nothing disturbed the quiet but the howling of a distant dog, the buzzing of insects and Intef's heavy breathing. Ramose thought that many people probably worked in the area, tending the tombs and the temples around the pyramids. There was no one around, though. All the workers had returned to their homes for the night. Ramose was led by his captors towards the pyramid, which loomed eerily in the dark.

"Okay, Scribe," said Hori. "This is where you earn your keep."

"Since you've only given me a piece of dry bread and three dates, there can't be much for me to do."

"Don't get smart," said Hori pulling out the papyrus that he had shown Ramose on the boat. "Find the entrance to the tomb."

Ramose had guessed that the men were tomb robbers. He hated the idea of helping them, but at that moment he didn't think that he had a choice. He peered at the papyrus in the dim light of an oil lamp. "It says:

Read these words well, they will teach you.

If you disturb the great one's place of rest, you will feel the wrath of the gods.

If riches come to you by theft, they will not stay the night with you.

The greedy man will have no tomb.

He will be tortured for eternity by the spirits."

"Maybe this isn't such a good idea," said Seth, glancing around nervously.

"Don't worry about that stuff. It's just to scare us off," Hori said. "Get to the important bit. Where's the tomb entrance?"

Ramose read on.

"Seek the truth where you least expect it,"

"What's that supposed to mean?" asked Intef, his brow furrowed with confusion.

"Tomb entrances are always facing north, aren't they?" said Hori. "Aligned with certain stars."

Ramose nodded.

"So maybe the entrance is on the south face of the pyramid," said Seth.

Hori nodded. "Yes but where? What else does it say, Scribe?"

"It says:

The sun rises twenty and seven cubits from the east and climbs to a height of ten and five cubits."

"That must be the measurements to find the entrance," said Hori.

Ramose was sure he was right, but he didn't say anything. He was thinking about what the scroll had said about feeling the wrath of the gods. The tomb robbers were hurrying to the south side of the pyramid. Ramose reluctantly followed them.

The men measured out the distances that Ramose read out from the papyrus. Intef clambered up the side of the pyramid with the aid of a rickety ladder that they made out of tamarisk branches and reeds. Intef had a large stone hammer tied around his waist.

"There's no sign of a doorway," said Intef.

"Of course there isn't," snapped Hori. "It's a hidden entrance!"

"Are you sure this is where it is?"

"Twenty and seven cubits from the eastern corner. Ten and five cubits up the side, that's what it says isn't it, boy?"

Ramose nodded, feeling a wave of guilt at helping the criminals.

Intef took the hammer from his belt and with a mighty swing smashed it into the side of the pyramid. The sound seemed deafeningly loud in the quiet of the evening. Ramose winced. The robbers listened anxiously to see if the noise had attracted anyone.

"It hardly made a mark," said Intef.

"It's solid stone," said Seth impatiently. "It's going to take more than one whack to break it."

Intef swung the hammer again and again. It took a dozen blows before the stone block even cracked. It looked like the ladder might give way before he broke it. The big man continued to swing the hammer, grunting louder with the exertion of each blow. His body glistened in the moonlight as the sweat ran down him.

"This is getting nowhere," he called down.

"That's because you're useless," Hori shouted. "Do I have to come up and do it myself?"

Even though Intef was plainly stupid, he didn't like anybody saying so. He swung his hammer with a growl of anger. The stone exploded under the blow, pieces of rock showered down on those watching below.

"That's more like it," said Hori with an ugly grin, aware that his jibe had worked.

"Don't get too excited," said Intef. "There's another layer underneath that one."

"Well, you better get into it, otherwise it'll be daybreak and we'll still be on the outside."

The second layer was thicker but made of mud brick. With a lot of grumbling and a few more hefty blows, Intef's hammer disappeared inside the pyramid. Seth cheered.

"Shut up, you fool," said Hori. "We don't want to bring the temple guards over here. Get the lamps and the bag, Scribe. You're going in with him."

"What about you?"

"Seth and I will keep watch."

Seth smiled, relieved that he didn't have to go inside the pyramid. It was an ugly sight as the robber had hardly any teeth. Ramose tentatively put his foot on the shaky ladder and climbed to the hole, balancing an oil lamp in one hand and with a bag of tools over his shoulder.

The air from inside the tomb was cool and had a strange smell. It was escaping after being sealed inside for four centuries. While he had been waiting for Intef to break into the pyramid, he'd read the papyrus carefully. The pyramid contained the tomb of Pharaoh Senusret from long ago.

Ramose remembered the name from Keneben's lists of kings, which he'd had to learn off by heart back in the palace schoolroom. He crawled in through the hole gouged in the white limestone of the pyramid. He'd been a good pharaoh as far as Ramose could remember, known for irrigation systems and trade with foreigners. Ramose didn't like the idea of disturbing his tomb.

7

THE SECRETS OF THE PYRAMID

INSIDE THE PYRAMID a narrow passage sloped downwards. The walls were lined with plain limestone, not decorated with carvings as his father's tomb had been. He sighed. He should be on his way to his father now, not stumbling around inside a pyramid. He could see Intef ahead, with a coil of rope over one shoulder and the stone hammer swinging from his waist. The ceiling was low and the big man had to stoop. So this is what it feels like to be a tomb robber, Ramose thought to himself. He had always found it hard to believe such people really existed. People who were so greedy for gold that they were willing to risk severe punishments. He'd heard of tomb robbers having their ears and lips cut off. More often than not they were executed. And that was only in this world. In the afterlife, tomb robbers faced eternal oblivion. No growing wheat in the Fields of Reeds for them. He wondered how Osiris, the god of the underworld, would judge an unwilling tomb robber.

Ramose had been expecting to feel his usual fear of enclosed spaces, but he didn't. Perhaps it was because it was night, and the darkness inside the pyramid seemed like a continuation of the darkness outside. Perhaps it was because he was tired and hungry. He hadn't seen any daylight for two days. He felt as if everything that was happening wasn't real, as if it was a dream and therefore nothing to be afraid of. As he descended into the depths of the pyramid he felt a strange calmness, as if he was watching himself from somewhere else—somewhere where it was safe.

At the bottom of the sloping shaft there was a high-ceilinged chamber. Intef straightened up with a groan. He looked around, squinting in the dim light of his lamp. The chamber had been carefully lined with smooth limestone, but it was completely empty.

"Where's the sarcophagus?" he said.

Ramose smiled at the man's stupidity. "If it was that easy to find the actual burial chamber it would have been robbed ages ago."

Intef's brow creased.

"The architect who built this didn't want the tomb to be found. He probably designed it with hidden passages and dead-end tunnels. There could be traps."

"But you know all about it from the writing, don't you?"

"It's written in a sort of riddle."

Intef walked around the chamber feeling the solid limestone walls. "But there's no other way out of this room."

"Yes there is," said Ramose who was beginning to enjoy making Intef look foolish, which wasn't hard. He read from the papyrus.

"Allow thy soul to be raised up towards heaven.

This is the best and shortest road towards knowledge.

The way of knowledge is narrow.

You must become a low and creeping thing."

Intef stood with his head cocked on one side like a large and stupid dog.

Ramose held his lamp above his head. The

roof of the chamber was made of stepped slabs of stone so that it narrowed to a point.

"The entrance to the next tunnel must be up there somewhere."

Intef held his lamp up and looked up. With the light from both lamps they could just make out a small dark square. It was at least the height of four men above them.

"How will we get up there?" asked Intef.

Ramose shrugged. "Don't ask me, I'm just a scribe."

They went back up the entrance shaft and pulled up the ladder. Even with the ladder in place underneath the upper tunnel entrance, it was still well short. Intef roughly carved handholds in the stone as far as he could reach from the top of the ladder. Greed had made him fearless. He climbed up, gripping the holes he had gouged in the limestone wall. Ramose was expecting him to slip and fall at every moment. He didn't. The big man clambered up the sheer wall like an enormous spider. He reached a ledge and crawled onto it.

"Okay, Scribe," he said. "Your turn."

"But I'm shorter than you, I won't be able to reach the handholds you've made."

Ramose felt the end of a coil of rope drop on his head.

"Tie that around you," said Intef.

Ramose tied the rope securely around his waist and then climbed the ladder. When he reached the top, he felt himself being lifted into the air. Intef hauled him up as if he was a sack of grain, not worrying about how he banged against the stone. Ramose grabbed hold of the ledge and clambered up onto it. A new passage sloped up from the ledge they were standing on in the direction of the centre of the pyramid. It had a low ceiling, nothing more than a tunnel roughly carved through solid stone.

"You go first," said Intef.

Ramose knew it was pointless to argue. He got down on his hands and knees and started to crawl up the tunnel, like a creeping thing, just as the papyrus had foretold. He held his oil lamp in one hand; it was no easy task. Ramose could hear Intef complaining as he crawled along behind.

Ramose's calm began to fade. He suspected his lack of fear had only been the effect of the beer on an empty stomach. He was now starting to imagine the hundreds of mud bricks just above his head. The narrowness of the tomb was making him feel stifled. He kept crawling. He thought about his friends. He wondered what they had done when they woke up and found him gone. They had no gold or copper to exchange for food. He began to think that he'd misread the papyrus, that this was a blind tunnel leading nowhere. He wanted to turn around and crawl back out again, but he knew the tunnel would be blocked by Intef's sweaty body. Even if the robber wanted to, he couldn't turn around in the narrow tunnel.

Just when Ramose was starting to really panic, the tunnel came to an end. He emerged in a passage which ran at right angles to the tunnel. This passage was wider, higher and properly faced with smooth limestone. Ramose stood up and straightened his aching back with relief. Intef came crawling out of the tunnel, cursing the workmen who made it so narrow. He stood up and peered down the new passage.

"The burial chamber must be this way," he said walking eagerly down the passage.

"Wait," said Ramose. "Don't be in such a hurry." He studied the papyrus and read aloud.

"Woe unto the impatient man. The goddess of the celestial ocean draws you down to her waters."

"Oh, that's just flowery writing," said Intef as he hurried on down the passage. "Don't take…"

Intef stopped suddenly. He stood frozen. Ramose came up behind him and held out his lamp. Intef was standing on the edge of a vertical shaft. The toes of his sandals were hanging over the edge. The shaft was only two cubits across, but it was too wide to jump safely to the other side. Ramose could not see how deep it was. He picked up a small stone and dropped it. He waited. After what seemed like minutes, he heard a faint splash. He looked at Intef. The big man had a terrified look on his face, realising that he had very nearly plunged to his death.

"Don't bother to thank me," Ramose said.

Intef found his voice. "How do we get across?" he asked shakily.

Ramose walked back along the passage looking for something that would span the gap. He found a recess in the limestone wall and a plank of wood that a lazy tomb maker had left there centuries earlier. He looked at it doubtfully. He didn't know whether he was prepared to trust his weight to a four hundred-year-old plank. He didn't have any choice.

"Hurry up," Intef prodded Ramose in the back. "We must be close to the burial chamber now."

Ramose lowered the plank over the gap. Intef loaded him up with the coil of rope and the bag of tools. He put his foot on the plank. He was glad he couldn't see the drop. He took one tentative step. The plank creaked. He took another step and it sagged in the middle. Ramose took two more steps, his heart racing, and he was over. Intef looked across at him.

"I don't know if it'll hold your weight," Ramose said. "Why don't I go on ahead and see if it's worth the risk?"

"Oh, no you don't." Intef didn't trust Ramose. "You could pocket half the gold."

"Okay. Come across then."

The big man took a breath and ran towards the gaping shaft. His full weight hit the middle of the plank. It cracked. He lunged forward as the ancient wood broke. He grasped hold of the rock ledge on the other side, his legs dangling down into the shaft. His feet scrabbled on the rock face but couldn't find anything that would support him. His hands clawed at the ledge. He started to slip.

"Help me," shouted Intef, his voice was high pitched with fear.

Ramose heard the broken pieces of plank hit the water far below with a faint splash. It seemed like they'd been falling for hours. He watched Intef's big, ugly hands grasping at the rock. For a split second, he thought about pushing the robber into the shaft, but instead he reached out and grabbed Intef under the arms. The man found a rock protrusion with his foot and levered himself up. Ramose hauled him onto the ledge.

"You knew that wouldn't hold my weight," grumbled Intef as he got to his feet.

Ramose was looking down into the shaft and wondering how they would get back over it again.

Intef's lamp bowl had broken when he fell, so they now had only one lamp between them. They walked along the passage which was sloping down slightly until it suddenly divided into two. Ramose held the lamp up to the papyrus scroll.

"The next bit is torn," he said. "I don't know which is the right passage."

"We'll take this one," said Intef. "You go first."

Ramose entered the right-hand passage. It twisted and turned. Up until then, Ramose had been able to keep a picture in his head of the way they had come. He'd still had a sense of which way north lay and where the burial chamber should be. After the passage had made six or more turns, he had no idea which way he was facing. The oil in the lamp was running low. Intef topped it up from a jar in his bag. They followed the passage for another three turns. Then it ended abruptly.

"You did that on purpose, didn't you?" said Intef. "You knew this was the wrong passage."

Ramose wasn't listening. He was sniffing.

"Can you smell something?"

He felt a burning in his throat. He looked down at his feet. They were almost buried in a fine yellow powder which covered the floor. Clouds of the powder had been kicked up as they'd walked around.

Ramose put his hand over his mouth and ran back along the passage. Intef followed him. Ramose felt dizzy. When he reached the fork in the passage he vomited. Intef was looking ill.

"What was that?" said Intef, taking a swig of his water. The big man's face had a greenish colour in the dim light.

Ramose retched again. "It must have been some sort of poison."

Intef reluctantly handed his water container to Ramose.

They retraced their steps and took the other passage which sloped down at a greater angle. Ramose thought they must now be down below ground level. He was still feeling sick and dizzy, but he hoped the poison had lost its potency over the centuries. The passage twisted and turned just as the other one had. Suddenly it opened into a chamber. It was exactly the same as the first chamber they had entered, high-ceilinged, lined with limestone—and completely empty.

Intef threw the coil of rope onto the floor. "You've led me astray again!"

Ramose sat down groggily. "Why would I do that? My father is dying in Memphis. I just want to get out of here."

Intef took another swig of water.

"This looks like the burial chamber," Ramose said looking around in the dim light. "Look at how smooth the limestone on the walls is. And see that niche?" He held the lamp over to one side lighting a recess cut into the wall. "That's where the Canopic chest would fit."

"So what are you saying?" said Intef chewing on a piece of dried meat. "They went to all the trouble of building this pyramid and then didn't use it?"

"That's a possibility. It might be nothing more than a giant hoax to lure tomb robbers away from the real tomb which is hidden somewhere else."

"What a dirty trick!" said Intef, spitting out bits of dried ox flesh.

Ramose didn't really believe that was the case at all. He didn't want the robbers to get the old pharaoh's gold and jewels. He thought about trying to convince Intef that the pyramid was empty, but he knew Hori wouldn't let him go until they found some treasure. If the tomb robbers didn't find it in the pyramid, they would have him digging holes all around it, looking for secret tombs. He had to get this over and done with so that he could get to Memphis and see his father. Ramose stood up again and walked around the chamber, looking closely at the walls and the ceiling in the dim light of the oil lamp. He studied the papyrus again. There had to be a clue.

The nut doesn't reveal the tree it contains.
The ignorant man doesn't see the truth
Though he treads upon it with his sandals.

Ramose dropped down onto his hands and knees and set the lamp on the stone floor. He ran his hands over it as if he was looking for something small that he'd lost. Intef looked as confused as ever.

"Here," said Ramose. He'd found what he was looking for. "Bring the lever over here."

For once, Intef didn't argue. He took a lever made of hardwood from his bag.

"There's a gap here. See?" Ramose brushed the dust away and ran his fingers around in a square. "It's a trapdoor."

8

THE DEAD PHARAOH

T HE LEVER was too thick to fit into the groove. Intef, impatient to get to the gold that he was sure was inside the tomb, got out his stone hammer and started to bash the slab of stone. The slab was thinner than the one that had covered the entrance to the pyramid. It was also horizontal, which made it easier for Intef to let the weight of the hammer do all the work. The slab soon cracked, then it broke into several pieces which disappeared from view and crashed to another floor not far below.

Ramose held the lamp down. The light reflected off gold in all corners of a chamber. Intef eagerly lowered himself down the hole, falling awkwardly on the floor three cubits below.

"This is it!" he exclaimed, limping around the chamber. "Look at all this!"

Ramose peered down the hole. He didn't know whether to be pleased or not. At one end of the chamber was a huge red granite sarcophagus. It was five cubits in length and three cubits high. All around the room there were chests covered with gold foil and pieces of furniture inlaid with jewels. Intef pushed a chest under the hole and balanced an elegantly carved chair inlaid with turquoise on top of it.

"Get down here with that lamp," he ordered.

Ramose clambered down. Intef was flinging open the lids of chests, laughing and exclaiming over all the jewellery, bowls and goblets he found within them. His face shone with the light reflecting from all the gold.

"This is just the beginning," he said turning to the sarcophagus.

"Can't we just take this stuff and leave the pharaoh in peace?" pleaded Ramose. "There's enough here to keep the three of you rich for the rest of your lives. More than enough. You don't need any more treasure."

Intef wasn't listening. He was trying to lift the lid from the sarcophagus. It was obviously impossible. The lid was made of solid granite two palm-widths thick. He pushed its edge with all his might.

"You can't push it off, Intef," said Ramose. "It'll be fitted inside the sarcophagus. You'll have to lift it."

Intef had another idea though. He climbed back up the hole and brought down his stone hammer. With a loud grunt he swung the hammer as high as he could and brought it down on the lid with all his strength. Ramose thought of the long-dead tomb makers and all the trouble they'd gone to in order to keep their pharaoh's resting place secret. They had built his sarcophagus with skill and care. It wasn't going to give up its treasure easily.

Intef continued to swing his hammer at the lid. He broke off a corner. Encouraged by this he smashed the hammer down on the broken edge. Intef furiously rained blows on the corner of the sarcophagus. Ramose sat on a chest and watched. He couldn't help thinking that if Intef used all that energy on something constructive, he'd be a lot better off. Eventually, after more than half an hour, the big tomb robber stopped and rested his hammer on the floor. He was gasping for breath and sweat was running down his back. There was a jagged hole in the end of the sarcophagus lid.

"That should do it," panted Intef.

Ramose looked puzzled. "You still won't be able to lift it off."

"I won't have to." Intef smiled unpleasantly. "You're going to get inside and bring everything out."

Ramose looked at the hole with horror. It was just about big enough for him to wriggle through. "I can't go in there," he said, starting to sweat despite the cool air of the tomb. "I...I'm not very good in enclosed spaces."

"Too bad." Intef lifted Ramose up and put him on top of the sarcophagus as if he was no heavier than a handful of figs. "Get on with it. We've got to get out of here before daylight."

Ramose threaded his legs in through the hole in the granite sarcophagus. His feet rested on the coffin. Ramose opened his mouth, and then closed it again. He knew there was no point in arguing.

"Give me the lamp."

Intef handed him the lamp. Ramose took a deep breath and lowered himself into the sarcophagus. The coffin was large and roughly human-shaped. It was decorated with beautiful patterns and a painting of the sky-goddess Nut with her wings outspread. Even in the dim lamplight, Ramose could see that the colours were as bright as if they were newly painted. He found it hard to believe that the coffin was four hundred years old. There was just enough room for Ramose to straddle the foot of the coffin.

"Do you want this?" asked Intef pushing the hammer through the hole.

"No," said Ramose. "I don't have to break it open. I can get the lid off."

It wasn't that easy though. He tried to get his fingers under the lid. It was jammed on tight. The carpenters who had made the wooden coffin had made the lid a perfect fit. They had never intended that anyone would be opening it.

"We haven't got time, just smash it open." Intef was getting impatient.

"Just let me try with a chisel first."

Intef handed him a chisel and Ramose fitted it in the crack between the lid and the base of the coffin. He wriggled it up and down, making the crack wider.

"Hurry up."

Ramose eventually eased the lid off. It parted from the coffin base with a sigh. Ramose pushed the lid over to one side.

The first thing he noticed was the smell. It smelt just like the embalming room under the temple where he had woken up after his nanny and tutor had faked his death. It was the strong resinous smell of juniper oil and frankincense. He held up the lamp. Inside the coffin was the pharaoh's mummy. A gilded mask stared up at him with blank eyes. The pharaoh's face had a strong nose and a mouth that was almost smiling. He'd always imagined mummies bound in soft white linen strips, but the bandages on the mummy in front of him were brown with age and stiff with the oils, long since dried up, that the priests had poured onto it during the burial ritual.

"Are there jewels? Is there gold?"

"Yes."

Ramose's lamplight reflected on a magnificent gold collar draped around the neck of the mummy and a gold crown on its head. The collar was made of hundreds, maybe thousands of beads of turquoise, carnelian, lapis lazuli and gold.

Ramose hesitated for a moment. Would he suffer the fate of a tomb robber if he was caught? And what about in the afterlife? Would Osiris understand that he'd had no choice? He pulled the collar from the mummy. The beautiful pattern disintegrated and the beads cascaded into the bottom of the coffin.

"What's going on in there?"

"The threads stringing the beads are rotten. Give me a bag."

Ramose scooped up beads by the handful and put them into the bag that Intef handed him.

The threads of the armbands broke as well. He scooped those beads into the bag with the others. Then he took off the crown. It was solid gold with a snake's head inlaid with turquoise rearing from the front as if to attack anyone who dared harm the pharaoh. Intef thrust a sharpened flint through the hole.

"Cut open the bandages. There'll be amulets wrapped inside."

Ramose didn't argue. He slit the bandages binding the mummy down the front and peeled them back. Sure enough there were exquisite amulets made of gold and precious stones. There was a heart scarab of lapis lazuli, similar to his own.

"Check the hands as well. There should be rings."

Ramose slit open the linen strips binding the hands to get to the dead pharaoh's fingers. The skin was like dried-out leather. The fingers were like black claws. Each one had at least one ring on it. As Ramose hurried to get the jewels, one of the fingers broke off in his hand. Until then, Ramose hadn't had time to think about his fear of enclosed spaces. Touching the actual withered flesh of the dead pharaoh made his stomach lurch and his heart pound. He was suddenly aware that he was inside a stone tomb, straddling a dead man. Above him was a mountain of stone and mud bricks. The fumes of the embalming resins were making his head spin. He threw the bag out of the hole and scrambled to get out of the sarcophagus.

"What's the rush all of a sudden?"

"Got to get outside."

Intef grabbed him by the arm and took the lamp from him, setting it down safely on the lid of the sarcophagus. "You're not going anywhere yet."

Ramose tried to struggle out of Intef's grasp. "I can't breathe. I need air. Fresh air. I have to get out."

Intef slapped him hard on the face with the back of his hand. "We're not leaving until we've gone through these chests."

Intef opened all the chests one by one and took out everything of value.

Ramose's breathing slowed. He wouldn't get out of the pyramid if he panicked. If Intef hadn't slapped him, he might have gone charging up the passage, fallen down the shaft and drowned in the celestial waters, or taken a wrong turn and ended up back in the poisonous yellow powder.

"Now get up to the upper chamber and I'll hand this all to you."

It was a slow business, but at the sight of the treasure Intef's impatience had completely disappeared. He handed the items one by one to Ramose, up through the hole in the ceiling of the burial chamber. Ramose, in the darkness of the upper chamber had no choice but to do as he was told.

"We'll need something to make a bridge across the gap as well," Intef looked around the chamber. There was a tall shrine in one corner of the chamber. It had two doors covered with delicately patterned gold foil. Inside was a wooden statue of the goddess Hathor. Intef grabbed hold of one of the doors and ripped it from its hinges. Ramose winced at the destruction of such a beautiful thing. He handed that up to Ramose as well. Finally Intef came up himself with the lamp.

There were four sacks of treasure. Intef carried three and gave one to Ramose to carry. They retraced their steps. Laying the shrine door across the shaft, they crossed the dark space. Then they crawled through the tunnel, Intef hauling his three sacks behind him.

It seemed to take forever. Ramose just kept thinking of the air and the space outside. Every step he took, every finger-width he crawled, brought him closer to it. He followed the dim light and Intef's grunts. The smell of the robber's sweating body just in front of him made him retch, but he kept going. Eventually they reached the end of the tunnel and climbed down to the false burial chamber. As he walked up the final passage, Ramose saw a dark blue square ahead of them, tinged with pink. It was the entrance to the passage. It was almost daybreak.

Hori and Seth were waiting impatiently.

"What took you so long?" called Hori as Intef thrust the ladder out of the hole in the pyramid and climbed down it.

Intef didn't say anything but threw down the four sacks of treasure. Ramose could hear the greedy sounds of the men gloating over their haul as he climbed down the rickety ladder. His legs were trembling. He was exhausted, parched and hungry. He collapsed on the ground.

"We had a visitor while you were away," said Hori with a smirk.

Ramose realised there was another figure in the group. Someone with his hands and feet tied. It was Hapu.

9

THE TOMB OF THE PRINCESS

T HE TOMB ROBBERS took their treasure and their prisoners back to the hiding place in the abandoned tomb. While Hori and Seth were poring over the pharaoh's treasure, Ramose sat with Hapu. Hori was so pleased with the haul that he'd given Ramose some dry bread and fish to eat. Ramose was still feeling sick, but he ate some of the food.

"I didn't know what to think when I woke up and you were gone," said Hapu. Now that they were back inside the temple, the tomb robbers had untied him.

"You thought I'd gone on to Memphis without you?"

"It did cross my mind, but when Karoya found that Mery was missing, she was convinced something was wrong."

"I would never have left you without food."

"That's what Karoya said. And no boats would have passed during the night, so we knew you must have gone inland."

"How did you find out where I was?"

"A boy minding pigs told us he'd heard the sound of men swearing during the night and Karoya found some footprints in the sand so we knew which direction you'd taken. Once we saw the pyramids, we guessed that's where they'd be heading. I wanted to search the temples. Karoya thought they'd be more interested in the tombs." Hapu looked guilty. "We had an argument. She went towards the pyramids and I started searching the temples. Hori saw me and captured me last night."

"So Karoya doesn't know where you are?"

"No."

Their conversation was interrupted by the sound of eerie wailing coming from just outside the tomb door. Seth looked up from the treasure in fear.

"What was that?"

"Just some sort of wild animal," said Hori.

"It sounds like a ghost to me, Seth," said Ramose.

Hapu smiled grimly. "What are we going to do?" he whispered to Ramose.

Ramose sighed. They had to get away from the tomb robbers. He knew he had to come up with a plan, but his mind wasn't working. He hadn't slept for two nights and he couldn't think straight.

"I have to get some sleep," he said to Hapu. He wrapped his cloak around him and lay down.

When Ramose awoke, the tomb robbers were preparing for another robbery.

"There are other tombs close to the pyramid," Hori said to Ramose.

"It doesn't say anything about other tombs on the papyrus," said Ramose trying to put Hori off. The last thing he wanted was to have to go down into another tomb.

"I found the entrance to one yesterday while you were in the pyramid. You wouldn't lie to me about what's in the papyrus, would you?"

"No. I told you, the papyrus is just about the pyramid."

"Well, you and your friend are going down into this tomb anyway, just as soon as it gets dark."

"You better let us out of here immediately," said Hapu. "You don't realise who Ramose really is."

"He's an apprentice scribe," said Intef looking puzzled.

"No he isn't. That's just a disguise," replied Hapu. "He's Prince Ramose, Pharaoh's son."

"I'm not stupid, you know," said Intef. "Prince Ramose died last year, everyone knows that."

"We were thinking of robbing his tomb, but there were still too many people in the valley," said Hori.

"He didn't really die. It was all a trick. This is him."

Hori nodded. "I'm actually a vizier. Did you know that? And Intef is a high priest. We're all in disguise." The tomb robbers all laughed at the joke. Seth suddenly let out a yell.

"There's a rat in the food bag," he said throwing the bag across the room.

"Is it alive?" asked Intef.

"I think it's dead."

Hori went over and prodded the bag. He opened it cautiously with a stick. Inside the bag among the temple offerings that they had stolen, was a dead rat.

"It must have been poisoned by the tomb bread," said Intef.

"It didn't die of poisoning. Something has killed it. See? It's bleeding."

The rat was still limp and bleeding from a wound in the neck.

"Do spirits have teeth?" asked Seth anxiously.

"Don't worry about it. Let's get going."

Intef grumbled all the way to the pyramid. "I'm not going down into another tomb. I hurt my ankle last night."

When they reached the pyramid, they walked around to the western side. Beyond the wall around the pyramid, outside the row of trees, there was an untended rocky area. Hori and Seth went over to a pile of rocks and started throwing them aside.

"Don't just stand there," Hori said to Ramose and Hapu. "Help." He turned to Intef. "You too."

They moved the pile of rocks and underneath they found a flat stone slab. Hori handed Intef the lever and the big man lifted the slab and pulled it aside.

Ramose smelt the same strange smell of ancient air as he had at the pyramid. He held up a lamp and looked down the shaft. It was a sheer drop.

"There's no ramp," he said. "The shaft's at least sixty cubits deep. How will you get down?"

"I'm not going down," said Hori. "You two are."

Hapu looked alarmed. "By ourselves?"

"No, don't worry, I'll send Seth down to hold your hand."

Seth didn't look happy. "Do I have to go down?"

"Intef's hurt his ankle. It's your turn to go down."

Ramose didn't bother arguing. He slung the bag containing tools and lamp oil over his shoulder. Intef tied the rope around Ramose's waist. The big man took a firm hold of the rope and braced himself. He nodded to Ramose. Ramose heard Hapu gasp as he stepped out into the dark hole, trusting the weight of his body to Intef's strong hands. He swung free. The big tomb robber grunted as he slowly lowered Ramose down the shaft. As he descended into the coolness of the tomb, Ramose felt the same dreamlike calm come over him as he had when he had entered the pyramid. He was getting used to being in tombs. It was almost as if he preferred them. He hadn't seen daylight in three days. He'd forgotten what it was like. Darkness was normal.

Hapu was lowered down next and then Seth. The boys held out their lamps to see what was around them.

"What do you see?" Hori's voice echoed down the shaft.

"Is there gold?" Intef shouted eagerly.

"There's just a tunnel," Seth shouted back. "We'll see where it leads." He started forward and then changed his mind. "You go first," he said.

The boys walked slowly along the tunnel. It was a rough-hewn passage, but not as low as the tunnel in the pyramid. Ramose and Hapu could walk along it comfortably, if they bent their heads a little. Seth had to bend over double.

"We better watch out for those demons you read about," said Hapu.

"What demons?" said Seth trying to look in front of him and behind him at the same time.

"He's just joking, Seth," said Ramose. "There was nothing about demons on the papyrus."

A noise echoed down the tunnel, the sound of falling rocks.

"What was that?" said Seth. He was so afraid, he almost grabbed Ramose's arm.

"It was just some stones falling down the shaft."

"It sounded like it was coming from the tunnel."

"It's an illusion. The sound echoes from one wall to another."

"I'm not so sure," said Hapu. "It could be the ghost of the owner of this tomb."

Seth stopped to listen. Hapu grinned at Ramose.

"Don't worry, Seth. We'll protect you."

The passage turned first to the left and then to the right and then opened into a chamber stacked with burial goods. Another short passage led to the burial chamber. The room was almost filled by a white sarcophagus. There was less than a cubit of space on either side. In each of the side walls there was a recess, stacked with chests. Seth's fear of ghosts suddenly evaporated.

"That was easy," he said, examining the lid of the sarcophagus. "I think we should be able to lift this and slide it off."

He was right. The lid wasn't as thick as the pharaoh's had been. With the aid of the lever, the three of them were able to lift the sarcophagus lid and then slide it over to one side. Ramose looked inside. There was a painted coffin similar to the one in the pyramid. Ramose held his lamp up to read the inscriptions.

"It's the tomb of a princess," he said. "Daughter of the pharaoh in the pyramid."

Seth had already jumped inside the sarcophagus and was smashing the coffin with the stone hammer.

"You don't have to break it," said Ramose. "We can ease it off."

"This is quicker," said Seth.

In a few minutes he had broken open the coffin. The mummy inside was small. The gilded mask bore the face of a young girl, a child. Seth was gleefully ripping the jewelled collar from around her neck and the armbands from her arms. The threads broke, just as they had with the pharaoh's jewellery. Seth scooped up handfuls of beads. He ripped the linen bindings from her and began roughly pulling the amulets from the mummy's body.

"Don't just stand there!" shouted Seth stuffing the treasure in a bag. "Start going through the chests and take anything valuable to the bottom of the shaft."

Ramose and Hapu did as they were told. They collected up golden bowls and goblets and alabaster vases and carried them to the shaft. Intef let down a large leather bucket on the rope and they piled the treasure into it to be hauled up. Inside one of the chests, Hapu found a casket decorated with gold and ivory. He opened it up. A sweet perfume filled the chamber.

"Look at this," he said.

Inside was a gold mirror and two silver combs. There were small jars made of jasper and greenstone, which would have once been filled with perfumes and cosmetics. Hapu closed the lid and carried it out to the shaft. Ramose saw another casket with similar decorations. He opened the lid. It was full of jewellery. There was a necklace with large solid gold beads in the shape of lions' heads. Two matching beaded anklets had seated lions threaded on them. Another necklace was strung with gold cowry shells. There was also a delicate crown decorated with rosettes of gold and turquoise. It had thin gold streamers hanging at the sides and a rearing snake's head at the front, similar to the pharaoh's only smaller. There were armbands made up of hundreds of beads. Ramose knew that if he picked up the jewellery, the rotten strings would break and the beautiful necklaces would crumble into a jumble of beads at the bottom of the box.

Ramose shut the casket lid without touching the jewellery and sat down with a sigh. He looked at the carvings on the alabaster tomb. It was sculpted with images of the young princess. He ran his fingers over the carved hair and the folds of her robes. She reminded Ramose of his sister, Hatshepsut. He wished he could do something to save the princess from the indignity of having her tomb stripped. He heard the sound of Seth grunting back down the passage.

Ramose jumped to his feet and looked around. There was a recess in the wall. It was packed full of furniture. He quickly pulled out the furniture and put the jewellery casket as far back as he could. There was some builder's rubble in the corner. He scooped it up and covered the casket. He picked up a gold painted chair and a stool just as Seth entered.

"Get a move on!" he shouted.

"I was just waiting for you to come back," said Ramose. "There's only room for one person at a time in the passage."

"Why are you bothering with all these chairs

and stools?" said Seth angrily. "They aren't worth much. I'll take out any jewels or gold inlaid in them. There should be more jewellery somewhere. Keep searching."

An hour later, Seth had stripped the tomb of everything of value. He had gouged out all the gold and jewels inlaid in the chests and furniture, leaving a pile of broken pieces of wood in the middle of the chamber. Ramose looked at the destruction sadly. At least Seth hadn't found the hidden jewellery casket, he'd been able to do that much for the princess.

They made their way back along the low-ceilinged passage. Seth was at the front. He stopped suddenly. "Look at this," he said holding up his lamp. "There's another passage."

Sure enough, hidden by a sharp turn in the passage was another opening that they hadn't noticed before.

"You go through and see if it leads anywhere," said Seth pushing Ramose into the passage.

"It's lined with smooth white limestone."

"It must lead to another tomb," said Seth excitedly. "They wouldn't have gone to that much trouble for a false tunnel."

"They might have. I'll just look at the papyrus."

"I thought you said the papyrus was only about the pyramid?" said Seth.

"It is," said Ramose hastily. "But there might be clues."

Seth's dirty hand reached out and grabbed the papyrus. He studied it in the lamplight.

"You can't read!" said Ramose. "You can stare at it as long as you like it won't make any sense to you."

Seth grabbed Ramose by the hair and shook him angrily. "You tell me what it says or I'll—"

"Look!"

Hapu had moved down the passage holding his lamp high. The light from it reflected on something further ahead.

Seth let go of Ramose, held up his own lamp and followed Hapu. In a niche halfway along the passage was a beautiful golden statue of the god Amun with a ram's head. It was studded with jewels and shone in the lamplight.

"That must be solid gold," said Seth pushing past Hapu.

"I can't believe it's been here for hundreds of years," Hapu said gazing at the statue. "It looks like it's just been polished."

Ramose was reading the papyrus.

"Does it say anything about this tomb on there?" Hapu asked quietly.

"Yes," whispered Ramose. "It refers to several other tombs. I just didn't want the tomb robbers to find them."

Ramose read on. He had an uneasy feeling. "Don't touch the statue, Seth," he called out to the robber. It says here:

He who offends Amun will feel the breath from the lord of eternity's nostrils. The fist of Osiris will descend to end his hour."

Seth wasn't listening. His eyes were sparkling with the light reflected from the statue. "That will melt down into enough gold ingots to last a lifetime."

Seth was so entranced by the shining object that he'd forgotten that Ramose had said there was nothing about the tomb on the papyrus.

Ramose looked anxiously around the passage. He noticed a dark patch in the ceiling above them. There was a black slot about four palm-widths wide, where a hole had been cut in the smooth limestone from one side of the passage to the other. Seth dropped his bag and reached out for the statue with both hands. Hapu leaned closer to look at the beautiful patterns made with inlaid jewels.

"Don't!" yelled Ramose.

Seth grasped the statue. There was a sudden rush of air from above. Seth and Hapu stood frozen.

Seth looked up. A huge slab of stone thundered from out of the slot above him. Ramose grabbed

Hapu and pulled him aside. He closed his eyes as the slab crashed to the floor with a deafening thud. Seth didn't even have time to scream.

Ramose opened his eyes. Hapu was sprawled on the floor. His foot was a finger-width from where the huge stone had fallen. He opened his mouth, but nothing came out.

Ramose gasped in horror.

A dismembered arm lay on the floor. Blood was trickling from it. That was all that was left of Seth.

"The fist of Osiris," whispered Ramose.

Clutched in the dead hand was the crumpled papyrus. Ramose reached over, prised open the warm fingers and took the scroll. All three lamps were lying broken on the passage floor. One wick was still burning with a spluttering light in a pool of oil.

Ramose picked up one of the lamps, which still had some of the bowl intact. He reached for Seth's bag and took out the flask of oil and filled the lamp as far as he could. He then carefully lifted the burning wick from the floor and put it in the broken lamp. Hapu was shaking uncontrollably. Ramose helped his friend up and together they made their way back to the bottom of the shaft.

"What's taking you so long down there?" said Hori as soon as he could see them.

"There's been an accident," said Ramose.

"Where's Seth?"

"He…he's dead."

The boys looked up. It was still dark outside. All they could see were two specks of light coming from Hori and Intef's lamps.

"What did you do to him?"

"We didn't do anything," said Hapu, close to tears.

"Where's the papyrus?"

"Seth had it. It's under the stone with him." Ramose folded the papyrus and stuffed it into his kilt.

"What stone?"

"It was the fist of Osiris. It crushed him."

"More like you've killed him and hidden the papyrus so you can come back later."

"We didn't! Come down and see for yourself. Seth has been crushed by a stone slab. It was a trap."

"Put the papyrus in the bucket."

"I can't, I haven't got it any more."

"Pull up the rope, Intef."

"Don't leave us down here," Hapu cried out.

"You were only useful while we had the papyrus. We would have had to get rid of you eventually anyway."

The rope was hauled up.

"No!" yelled Hapu. "Don't leave us here."

Ramose grabbed at the rope but he was too late. It disappeared up the shaft. There was a dull thud as the slab above was lowered into place.

10

UNDERGROUND

THE TWO BOYS stood looking up the dark shaft. "They'll come back for us, won't they?" asked Hapu. "They won't leave us to die here."

"Yes they will."

Hapu turned angrily to Ramose. "Why didn't you give them the papyrus?"

"It wouldn't have made any difference," said

Ramose grimly. "You heard what Hori said. They were planning to kill us anyway. He didn't want to risk us telling someone about their theft. They're tomb robbers, Hapu. There's no worse crime. Leaving a couple of apprentices to die is nothing compared to stealing gold from the body of a pharaoh." Ramose shuddered at the memory of the old pharaoh's black, leathery skin and his claw-like fingers.

Hapu slumped to the floor. "I don't want to die."

"Neither do I," replied Ramose. "Perhaps there's another way out."

"There was, but it's blocked with a slab of stone that twenty men couldn't lift."

"We'll have to look for another."

"You've still got the papyrus, did it say there was another entrance?"

"The papyrus isn't that clear."

"So what was the point of writing it if it doesn't make sense?"

"It's a puzzle. Whoever wrote it was giving directions for breaking into the pharaoh's tomb, but it's as if he knew it was wrong and he wanted to make it as difficult as possible."

"We're going to die," Hapu said, his voice was getting higher. "We're going to slowly starve to death." He turned to Ramose with a panicked look in his eyes. "And it's your fault. You should have given them the papyrus. They might have pulled us up. You could have made up a story about another tomb full of treasure."

Ramose ignored his friend's accusations.

"The papyrus mentions other tombs. There might be a connecting passage."

"Does it say there's a connecting passage?"

"No," said Ramose. "We just have to hope there is. Come on, we're wasting lamp oil sitting here feeling sorry for ourselves. Let's start searching."

Ramose picked up the broken lamp and headed down the passage towards the princess's tomb. As he walked along the passage, he examined the walls, the ceiling and the floor in the lamplight. Hapu walked behind him snivelling.

They reached the burial chamber. Ramose stepped over the pile of broken furniture that Seth had left behind and examined the walls of the recess where he had hidden the princess's jewellery casket. There were no openings. He went to the other recess and held up the lamp so that it lit the dark corners. There was nothing there either.

"That's it. We're stuck here," said Hapu leaning against the stone wall. "There's no other possible way out. Perhaps we were meant to die in the flood," he said. "You can't avoid death if that's what the gods want."

Hapu sounded calmer, as if he had accepted his fate.

Ramose thought of all the times he'd cheated death in the last year: the attempt to poison him back at the palace, his fall from the mountain, the flash flood. He wasn't about to surrender to death now. Ramose looked at the papyrus.

When day comes, how will tomorrow be?

Life or death we do not know what awaits us.

No man can alter the lifetime that has been granted to him.

The papyrus seemed to be agreeing with Hapu. He read the words over and over again until they lost their meaning and just looked like squiggles on the scroll. He looked into the flickering flame of the oil lamp. Ramose's mind went blank. He couldn't create thoughts in his head. The two boys sat for nearly an hour in silence.

Suddenly some words that he'd read earlier popped into the blank space in Ramose's head. *The good servant stands behind her mistress.* He jumped to his feet.

"We didn't look behind the sarcophagus," he said to Hapu. "I think the tomb of the princess's servant might be behind this tomb."

Hapu looked up at Ramose without understanding. The sarcophagus looked as if it was pushed up against the back wall of the chamber, but there was actually a space of about three palm-widths behind. Ramose held the lamp up and peered behind the sarcophagus. All he could see was solid stone wall. Then he noticed a small piece of linen caught under the bottom edge of the sarcophagus. Some unfortunate tomb worker must have got his kilt caught under it as it was lowered into place four hundred years ago.

Ramose held the lamp closer to the scrap of material. It was gently rising and falling as if a soft breeze was lifting it. Ramose got down on his knees and held his hand in front of the fragment of linen. There was a faint breath of air. He squeezed in behind the sarcophagus. He felt around with the toe of his sandal. Down at floor level there was an opening no higher than a stool. There was no room to bend down. Ramose placed his back to the sarcophagus and slid down. He could just get his knees into the hole. He stretched out his feet. It was a tunnel, small but the slight movement of air told him it had to lead somewhere.

"Hapu, come on. I've found a tunnel."

Hapu got up, still in a trance. He peered behind the sarcophagus and saw Ramose disappearing feet first into the wall. He came to life and was soon squeezing in after his friend.

The tunnel was very low. The boys had to

wriggle along on their backs pushing themselves along on their elbows. It wasn't easy. The tunnel was only a few cubits long though. Ramose soon found himself in another chamber. He scrambled to his feet and held up the lamp.

"There are two passages," he yelled. "One of them must lead somewhere."

Hapu wriggled out of the passage and got to his feet as well. The boys smiled at each other. Ramose could see his friend's teeth flash in the lamplight. There was still a hope. Then the lamp flickered and went out and they were plunged into darkness.

"There's more oil isn't there?" said Hapu, his voice starting to sound panicky again.

"Yes, there's oil, but we haven't got any way of making a flame."

"Where did the papyrus say this passage leads?"

"It didn't say anything. The rest of the scroll was torn off."

"What will we do?" Hapu seemed to think that Ramose could always come up with something.

"I don't know," said Ramose.

They stood in silence for a moment while the truth of their situation sunk in.

"We don't have a choice then," said Hapu. "We have to see where the passages lead."

Ramose nodded in the darkness even though he

knew Hapu couldn't see him. But the truth was he was beginning to lose hope. With the darkness all around him he suddenly felt the weight of the earth and stone above him. He felt as if it was crushing him. He gasped for breath, but he could not seem to get any air into his lungs. His legs crumpled underneath him.

"Ramose, what's wrong?"

Ramose sucked in quick, short breaths, but it didn't make any difference, he still felt like he was suffocating.

"Come on, Ramose," Hapu said, trying to pull his friend to his feet. "We have to feel our way along the passages. One of them has to lead somewhere. We can't give up."

Ramose didn't say anything, but his head was filled with thoughts of death. He'd been wrong before. He hadn't cheated death, he'd just postponed it. The gods wanted him in the underworld and nothing he could do could change that. He didn't have the power to defy the gods. He felt Hapu's hand grab his and pull him along the dark passage.

The right-hand passage was high enough for them to walk upright. With his free hand Hapu felt along the walls. It was a roughly carved passage and he tripped more than once on the uneven floor. Ramose allowed himself to be pulled along in a daze.

A change in the air around them told them that the passage had opened out into a larger chamber, but Hapu immediately bumped into something. He felt it with his hands.

"It's another sarcophagus," he said. "Just a rough stone one. It must be the tomb of the good servant you mentioned."

Hapu left Ramose by the sarcophagus and felt his way around the chamber.

"The tomb makers didn't waste too much time on the servant's tomb," he said. "The burial chamber's only just big enough to fit the sarcophagus. There's no space around it."

Ramose heard the sounds of Hapu feeling around the sarcophagus.

"There's nothing else here," Hapu said. "We'll have to go back and try the other passage."

He took Ramose's limp hand and led him back down the passage. The other passage was lower, forcing them to stoop.

"It has to lead somewhere," Hapu kept saying over and over, but Ramose could hear that his confidence was fading with every step.

Hapu stopped suddenly.

"There's a pile of stones," he said.

Ramose put out his hands in front of him. He felt the rough surfaces of large boulders piled on top of one another.

"The passage is blocked," said Hapu.

Ramose could hear the last of the hope drain from his voice.

Ramose reached up to the ceiling of the passage-way. The boulders were stacked right to the top and jammed in so tightly that none of them would move. Ramose sat down on the cold stone floor. He was tired. He was hungry. He was thirsty. He could hear Hapu next to him swallowing tears. Ramose was beyond tears. He closed his eyes even though it was dark. Behind his eyelids he could see little flashes of light and swirls of colour. He had forgotten what daylight was like. It was only three days since he'd been bathed in the heat and light of the sun by the river, but it seemed like a dim and distant memory.

He knew now that he would never see daylight again. It was the will of the gods. He would never see his sister, Hatshepsut glide into a room like a young goddess. He would never see the flash of Karoya's smile or hear her ringing laughter. His father would die—he may already be dead. Ramose would never be able to say goodbye. He would never take his father's place as pharaoh. He would never again see the slow, silent Nile and its rich, fertile valley.

Hapu had stopped crying. They were both waiting for death. Ramose remembered a passage from the papyrus.

Do not give in to the terror of thick darkness.
The heart is not made strong if it is not tested.
The light that guides you may be invisible.

It was as if whoever wrote the papyrus had known what would happen to them. But Ramose couldn't help but give in to the darkness. What choice did he have? Perhaps the invisible light would lead him to the afterlife.

Ramose opened his eyes. There was no difference whether his eyes were open or closed. He'd been sleeping. He had no idea for how long. It could have been a few minutes. It could have been many hours. He wondered how long it would take him to die, if it would be painful or if he'd just go to sleep again and never wake up. He was cold. He wished he had his cloak so he could at least die warm. He sat closer to Hapu, so that they could share what little body warmth they had.

Ramose woke suddenly. He'd dreamt that something soft and warm had brushed against his leg. A noise had awoken him. A loud animal sound.

He was definitely awake now, but he felt the sensation again on his chest. It took his breath away. He felt it brushing his face. He could smell something too. A fishy smell. There was another noise, a soft rumbling in his ear. Then he felt sharp teeth sink into his nose. Ramose sat up and reached out. His hands touched something warm, soft and mobile.

"Hapu," he said. His voice was hoarse. "Hapu, it's Mery."

Hapu stirred beside him.

Ramose stroked the cat from its nose to the tip of its long tail. He felt the earring in its left ear and the ceramic Horus eye amulet around its neck.

"It's not a dream, Hapu. She's real."

Ramose reached out and found his friend's hand and touched it on the cat's head. Hapu pulled his hand away as if he'd just dipped it in a pot of boiling water. He sat up. Ramose felt him tentatively reach out and touch the cat again.

"Are you sure we're not imagining her?" said Hapu croakily.

Mery miaowed.

"I'm sure," said Ramose feeling his mouth shape into a smile. "She bit me on the nose."

"How did she get here?"

"I don't know. We have to follow her."

"How can we do that in the dark?"

"She's the invisible light."

Ramose felt for the hem of his kilt. There was a small rip where he'd caught it on a sharp rock as he was lowered into the tomb. He tore it further until he had ripped a strip off the bottom of his kilt. He tied one end to the cat's collar.

"Okay, Mery," he said.

The cat started to clam

the passageway. Hapu

strip of linen. Ramose fel.

"Where's she gone?" he

come undone?"

"No," said Hapu. "I can still i

it."

Ramose moved his fingers along the length of linen. He rested his foot on one of the lower rocks so that he could lift himself up. The strip of linen disappeared through the stone barrier.

"Up here," he shouted, his fingers feeling the rocks in the top corner of the blocked passage. "There's a hole. It's tiny. Just small enough for Mery to fit through."

"That's no good for us."

"I can fit my hand through though." Ramose reached his hand through the small hole. From behind he could loosen a few small stones. They heard the sound of them clattering to the floor on the other side. Ramose strained, his feet were slipping off the smooth surface of the boulders.

"Help me up," he said.

Hapu knelt down so that Ramose could climb on his back. He reached his arm into the hole up to his armpit. He loosened more small stones, then a larger one about the size of a pomegranate fell away.

ge was blocked from the other side,"
ose, his breath coming in gasps. "I
be able to…" he strained and grunted.
out of the way!"

Ramose pushed a larger rock. It moved only
slightly. Ramose pushed again, the exertion was
making him feel faint. He gave the rock one
final shove and it tumbled into their side of the
passageway. Hapu reached up and pulled down
more rocks until there was a hole big enough for
them to wriggle through. They tumbled into the
passage on the other side.

"I've lost the linen strip," Hapu cried out. "I
don't know where Mery is."

Ramose was lying on the floor where he had
landed. He felt the cat nudge his arm. "She's
here!" He reached out and grabbed the linen
strip. "She's leading us. Come on!"

Ramose tried to get to his feet and bumped his
head on the passage ceiling. "This passage is very
low," he said. "We'll have to crawl."

He felt Mery tug on the linen strip and he
followed the cat on his hands and knees.

The passage continued on. Ramose's knees grew
sore. Then his knees bumped into something. His
hands were resting on a higher level. He felt
angular shapes. He knew this meant something,
but he'd been so long in the dark, he couldn't
picture what it was he was feeling.

Slowly an image formed in his mind.

"Steps!" he called out to Hapu. "There are steps leading up."

He raised his head and above him he could see something bright, something glaringly white. His eyes took a while to make sense of it.

"Daylight!" he said.

It was only a chink of light, but it was dazzling. Ramose stumbled up the steps. Hapu followed him. At the top, Mery disappeared through a small hole. There was a rectangular slab covering the shaft. Ramose and Hapu pushed at the slab. It didn't move. They could hear noises on the other side. The sound of someone moving rocks off the slab. The boys pushed again. The slab lifted a little, less than a finger-width. Someone pushed a stout piece of wood through the gap. With the help from above, the boys managed to lift the slab far enough so they could clamber out.

The light was blinding. Ramose couldn't open his eyes. A hand grabbed him and pulled him along. He stumbled forward. The ground began to slope down steeply. Ramose could hear the faint trickle of water. The glare softened and his skin grew cool. He knew they were somewhere shaded from the sun. He could see an image swimming in front of his eyes: a dark circle framed with red and green, and in the middle of it a bright white curve. It was Karoya's smiling face.

11

RETURN TO THE RIVER

KAROYA'S FACE wasn't smiling for long. "A temple guard discovered that the pyramid has been broken into," she said. "The temple workers are searching for thieves. We can't stay here."

"But we aren't tomb robbers," said Hapu.

"We're strangers with no reason to be here," said Ramose. "It would be hard to convince them."

The boys both took a deep drink of water from the waterbag that Karoya offered them. Ramose stroked Mery who purred loudly as if she was very pleased with herself. After the time of darkness, the cat's sandy stripes seemed bright and beautiful. Her green eyes were like jewels. She stepped into Karoya's lap, circled round and settled down to sleep.

"I don't want to ever hear you complaining about Mery again, Hapu," Karoya said.

"I won't. Never," said Hapu as he swallowed the last of the water.

"We have to get away from this place as soon as possible," Ramose said.

"We'll have to wait till night and then go back to the river." Karoya was anxious that they would be caught again.

"How can we travel by boat to Memphis?" asked Hapu. "We haven't got any gold."

"Yes we have," Karoya held up Ramose's bag. "I found the tomb robbers' hiding place."

Ramose opened his bag. Inside were the remaining rings of gold, his scribal tools, his cloak and his heart scarab. After Mery had emerged from the bag spitting and scratching, the robbers hadn't looked in it again.

Karoya produced bread and figs from her own bag. Ramose and Hapu ate hungrily. As his eyes slowly got used to light again, Ramose began to look around. They were in a marshy hollow where a small stream flowed. An outcrop of rock shaded them from the sun and, more importantly, kept them from being seen. Ramose couldn't believe how his luck had changed in the last couple of hours.

"We must get back to the river," he said. "I have to see my father."

They waited until the sun was setting before they started off again. Ramose watched the yellow disc sink behind the old pharaoh's pyramid, wishing it hadn't disappeared so quickly.

"Can't we sleep?" asked Hapu. "I'm so tired."

"We have to get as far away from here as we can," said Karoya. "Then you can rest."

Ramose couldn't remember anything about his journey from the river to the pyramid, but Karoya seemed to know where she was going, even in the dark. He was happy to let her lead.

After walking for an hour or so, Ramose could go no further.

"We have to rest, Karoya," he said.

Hapu groaned and slumped to the ground. Karoya found an empty grain store where they could sleep and they crawled inside. Ramose was asleep in seconds.

The next day, they decided they were far enough away from the pyramid to risk walking in daylight. They travelled through rough swampy ground and saw no one. By midday they were back on the banks of the river.

"We'll have to find a village," Ramose said. "There won't be any boats stopping here in the middle of nowhere."

They rested a while and then headed north along the river's edge. They reached a small village in the late afternoon. The villagers were finishing their work in the fields and walking back to a huddle of mud brick houses. A few simple reed boats were tied up to a wooden mooring platform. Ramose inquired about a boat, while Hapu and Karoya went in search of food.

"There's a farmer taking grain to Memphis," said Ramose when he returned to his friends. "But he isn't leaving till the day after tomorrow."

"Did he want to know who we were?"

Ramose nodded. "I told him the same story, we're apprentices sent to work in a temple in Memphis. Karoya is our slave. I said we'd argued with the captain of the naval boat we were on and been left behind to make our own way."

"Did he believe you?"

"I think so."

They sat down by the river's edge within sight of the place where the boats were moored. Karoya laid out the fish, lentils and fruit that she and Hapu had bought from a kindly woman. She gathered dry reeds and animal dung and made a small fire in the sand. She pulled the cooking pot from her bag. Ramose smiled. Through all their adventures, Karoya hadn't lost any of her things.

"The people are friendly in this village," said Karoya. "We can wait. Hapu, put some water in the pot."

"Yes, Your Highness," grumbled Hapu as he picked up the pot and took it to the water's edge. "How come you never ask Ramose to do your errands for you?"

Karoya opened her mouth to reply, when a sudden cry interrupted the argument.

"There they are!"

Ramose whipped round. The farmer he had spoken to was pointing at them. Behind him was a man dressed in the robes of a high priest.

"They're tomb robbers," shouted the farmer. An angry crowd of villagers and temple workers gathered and started to surge in their direction.

Hapu dropped the pot in the river and ran back to Ramose and Karoya. "Now what do we do?"

Ramose didn't know what to do. Karoya gathered up Mery and their food, ready to run.

"Don't run," said Hapu. "We can explain."

The villagers surrounded them and grabbed hold of Ramose.

"We're not tomb robbers," he said.

"Search his bag," said the high priest as he arrived, out of breath.

The farmer snatched Ramose's bag. He pulled out the gold rings and Ramose's ebony palette. The gold, ivory and turquoise glinted in the sunlight. The growing crowd muttered angrily.

"He is a thief!"

"That's my palette," said Ramose. "I'm a scribe."

"You're not old enough to be a scribe," said the high priest, "and what sort of apprentice scribe has a palette inlaid with gold and ivory? You must have stolen it from the tomb."

The priest pulled a linen bundle from Ramose's bag. He undid the wrappings and stared at the lapis lazuli scarab that lay in his hand.

"That's his," cried Hapu. "It belongs to him. He's not a tomb robber, he's not even an apprentice scribe, he's—"

"Shut up, Hapu," said Ramose.

The priest searched Ramose. He found the papyrus which was still tucked in the belt of his kilt. As he pulled it out, a shower of beads fell to the ground, released from a fold in his kilt where they'd been caught since the old pharaoh's collar had broken. The old woman who Karoya had bought the food from fell to her knees and picked up the beads.

"Turquoise and gold," she said turning to Karoya accusingly. Her face was no longer kindly.

"What more proof do you want?" shouted a

villager. "Look at that. Beads from a royal neck."

The priest was studying the papyrus. "This could be coded instructions for how to find the pharaoh's tomb inside the pyramid."

The crowd was surging forward, ready to grab the thieves. The priest was looking at Karoya.

"What's the slave girl got in that basket?"

He grabbed hold of the basket. Karoya refused to let it out of her grasp. Others grabbed her arms and she was forced to let go. The priest opened it and Mery sprung out hissing and spitting like a demon. She sunk her claws into the priest's chest and snarled in his face. The priest leapt backwards and dropped the heart scarab. The startled cat took one look at the angry people around her and leapt into the river. The villager holding Ramose loosened his grip.

"Look!" he said, pointing downstream.

The villagers and the high priest looked down the river. So did Ramose. A huge barge was sailing majestically into view. This was not a rough village boat, it was skilfully made from cedar wood. The prow and the stern turned up and were carved into the shape of papyrus stalks in flower. The boat was travelling south, so a white linen sail was billowing from a mast. Ramose wasn't looking at the structure of the boat though. He was already very familiar with it.

"It's the royal barge," he whispered.

He was staring at the people on board. Standing at the front of the boat with his bony, insect-like hands clasped behind him, his robes fluttering in the breeze, was Vizier Wersu. Sitting in a gilded chair eating grapes and being fanned by two of her servants was his sister, Hatshepsut. She was talking to a woman alongside her who was sipping from a golden goblet. The woman wore an elaborate wig topped by a crown. It was Queen Mutnofret. A young boy dangled a fishing line over the side. Three servants stood by watching him anxiously. It was Prince Tuthmosis, Ramose's half-brother.

As the boat glided effortlessly past, the breeze lifted a piece of reed matting that was protecting a cabin in the centre of the boat. An old man was sitting inside on a throne. Ramose gasped. The face was thinner than when he'd seen it last and the lines of age were deeper, but he knew the face well. It was his father. A young man made his way from the stern of the boat with a papyrus scroll under one arm and a palette and brush box in his other hand. He stopped next to the princess and bowed.

"Keneben!" Ramose called out the name aloud. The villagers were all falling to their knees and calling out blessings to their pharaoh. Ramose ran out into the river. "Hatshepsut! Keneben!" he called, but the breeze carried his words away and neither his sister nor his tutor heard him. Ramose kept wading out into the river, vainly trying to reach the barge. It was as if his whole life was slipping past in front of him. He should have been on the royal barge eating grapes, drinking wine. Instead he was struggling against the river, thin and exhausted, accused of being a thief even though he had nothing but the dirty, torn kilt that he was wearing.

"Wait," he called out, wading deeper. He lost his footing and the current of the river carried him away from the barge. He tried to swim towards it, but the barge was too fast, the river too strong. His family disappeared around the next bend in the river. Tears ran down Ramose's face and mingled with the waters of the Nile.

A cry from the shore brought Ramose back to his current situation. He remembered his friends. Karoya and Hapu were still on the riverbank. Now that the barge had passed, the villagers were getting to their feet.

"Karoya, Hapu, jump in the river," he called. "We have to swim to the other side'"

"I can't swim," Karoya called out.

"Yes, you can. I'll help you."

Hapu could see the villagers turning on them again. He grabbed Karoya by the hand and dragged her into the river. Ramose swam towards them. The villagers were following. Hapu threw himself into the water, pulling Karoya with him. He splashed around inexpertly, but managed to stay afloat. Karoya struggled and screamed and lost hold of Hapu's hand. She disappeared under the water.

Ramose swam to them and dived under the water. He could see Karoya, her eyes closed, her mouth open, struggling helplessly against the force of the water. He grabbed her under the arms and carried her to the surface. She was still trying to fight the water. She choked in air and water at the same time.

"Listen to me, Karoya," Ramose gasped. "We have to get to the other side of the river."

Karoya stared wildly at the wide expanse of water between them and the other bank. She shook her head furiously.

"Look," he said. "Mery's doing it."

The cat was swimming towards them in wide-eyed terror. "I'll help you. Just relax and you'll float, trust me."

People were clambering onto one of the reed boats. Ramose started to swim to the middle of the river. He held Karoya under her arms. She started to struggle again.

"Lie on your back," Ramose said. "Imagine you're lying on a soft straw mattress."

Ramose kicked out with his feet and felt the current carry them.

"Close your eyes so that you can't see the water," he said.

Karoya closed her eyes, her body relaxed a bit.

"Now kick gently."

Karoya kicked her legs. Ramose felt her body become more buoyant.

"See. You're not sinking. I have hold of you. It's safer here in the water than on the shore."

Mery swam over to Ramose and was trying to clamber up onto him. Karoya's cooking pot floated into view. Ramose lifted the cat up and put her inside the pot. Mery yowled miserably. Ramose pushed the pot in front of him with one hand while with the other he supported Karoya. He looked around for Hapu who was swimming across the river, splashing and gasping, but making progress. The river was wide. Ramose kept kicking his legs and reassuring Karoya. Eventually they reached the other side. All three crawled ashore, and collapsed on the wet sand. Mery jumped out of the pot and stalked onto the sand and shook herself indignantly.

Ramose lay on the wet sand, his breath rasping. "My father still lives," he said.

"May he have long life and happiness," gasped Hapu.

"I saw your sister," said Karoya. "She is more beautiful than ever."

"Did you see the young man on the barge?"

His friends nodded.

"That is Keneben, my tutor. It was he who saved my life when the queen tried to poison me. He's returned from Punt."

Ramose looked across the river. Some villagers were rowing towards them in a reed boat.

"We have to keep moving," he said.

"Where will we go?" asked Hapu, struggling to his feet.

"To the desert. They won't follow us there."

There was no farming on that side of the river. Papyrus reeds grew densely on the river's edge, beyond that there were wild grasses and acacias. The friends got to their feet and hurried into the undergrowth. They ran as fast as their fading strength would allow. They kept going until it was almost dark. With no irrigation canals to carry the river water inland, the vegetation thinned out quickly and they were soon in the sparsely vegetated land on the edge of the desert.

Ramose peered back into the dimming light.

"I don't think they've followed us," he said. "Egyptians don't like venturing into the desert."

They made a camp. Ramose collected fallen dates. Karoya gathered wild grain. Hapu managed to snare an ibis. Karoya made a fire and they were able to have a small but welcome meal.

They took stock of their situation. In the rush to get away they had lost most of their things.

"All we have is the cooking pot, a few deben of copper and a cat," said Hapu miserably. "Oh, and this." He pulled something from the belt of his kilt. It was Ramose's heart scarab. "The priest dropped it when he saw the royal barge." Hapu examined the jewel. "There's a chip out of it, but I thought you might still want it."

Ramose took the lapis lazuli scarab from his friend with a grateful smile. He fingered the hieroglyphs that spelt out his name.

"At least I still know who I am," he said.

"What are you going to do now, Ramose?" asked Karoya quietly.

Ramose had been thinking about that as they'd walked. He knew what he had to do.

"I'm going to follow my father back to Thebes. To tell him that his true heir lives and that he's ready to take the throne of Egypt."

Hapu shifted uncomfortably. "I sometimes forget that you're who you are," he said.

"You seem eager to tell everybody that we meet," grumbled Ramose.

"Yes, but seeing the royal barge and your sister again made me realise you might really be pharaoh one day."

"That's my plan. I'd started to think that it was impossible. Now that I know Father is still alive and that I have friends in the palace, I know it isn't."

Karoya smiled, looking at her ragged friend. "You don't look much like a pharaoh."

"I will one day."

"Do we have to go back to Thebes?" groaned Hapu. "We've just spent three weeks and risked our lives getting away from Thebes."

"That's where I'm going," said Ramose. "You don't have to come if you don't want to."

"Of course I'll come. But how will we get there? They took your gold."

"We can walk," said Karoya.

"Walk?" Hapu looked at her as if she was suffering from sunstroke.

"It'll take a while, but we'll get there. My people thing nothing of walking such distances."

"What will we eat? Where will we sleep?"

"We'll sleep under the stars as before."

"If we keep to the edge of the desert like this, no one will bother us."

"We can go back to the river every so often to fish," said Karoya. "There are dates and wild grains. We won't go hungry."

Ramose smiled at his friends. He'd come a long way since he'd been the spoilt prince in the palace. He could walk to Thebes. He had friends to help him. He also knew that his sister and tutor were waiting for him at the palace. He felt sure he could face whatever his future held.

"The gods will provide," said Ramose.

A WORD FROM THE AUTHOR

IT MIGHT seem to us that the ancient Egyptians were a strange lot. They spent a lot of their time thinking about death. They weren't a solemn or unhappy people though. They believed that when they died they would live on in an afterlife. During their lives they prepared their own tomb, making sure it contained everything they would need in the afterlife.

Thanks to these beliefs and the fact that many of the tombs were underground, a lot have survived. Even though tombs are all about death, they provide us with a lot of knowledge about the way ancient Egyptians lived.

The ancient Egyptians lived around three thousand years ago. I find it fascinating that we know so much detail about life so long ago.

Ramose was a real person. His father, Pharaoh Tuthmosis I lived from 1504–1492 BC. Some historians believe that his 'chief' wife bore him three sons who all died before the pharaoh. A son of a lesser wife therefore became the next pharaoh. No one knows what happened to Ramose and his brothers. I thought it would be interesting to imagine the reasons for the early deaths of the princes. That is how the Ramose stories came about.

GLOSSARY

akhet

The ancient Egyptians divided the year into three seasons. Akhet was the first season of the year when the Nile flooded.

amulet

Good luck charms worn by ancient Egyptians to protect them against disease and evil. Amulets were also wrapped inside a mummy's bandages to give good luck to the dead person as they travelled through the underworld.

canopic chest

When the ancient Egyptians mummified bodies, they removed most of the insides (except for the heart). They put the insides in jars and they were in turn put in a chest. This chest, called a Canopic chest after a town called Canopus, was placed in the tomb with the coffin.

carnelian
A red stone used in jewellery.

cowry shell
An oval-shaped sea shell. The ancient Egyptians used them as good luck charms.

cubit
The cubit was the main measurement of distance in ancient Egypt. It was the average length of a man's arm from his elbow to the tips of his fingers, 52.5 cm.

deben
A unit of weight somewhere between 90 and 100 grams.

Horus eye

Horus was the hawk-god of ancient Egypt. Horus lost an eye in a battle, but the goddess Hathor restored it. His eye became a symbol of healing and is used in many paintings and sculptures.

lapis lazuli

A dark blue semi-precious stone which the Egyptians considered to be more valuable than any other stone because it was the same colour as the heavens.

niche

A space or recess cut back into a wall, usually made to store something or to display a statue or a vase.

palm-width

The average width of the palm of an Egyptian man's hand, 7.5 cm.

papyrus

A plant with tall, triangular shaped stems that grows in marshy ground. Ancient Egyptians made a kind of paper from the dried stems of this plant.

peret

The season of spring.

sarcophagus

A large stone container, usually rectangular, made to house a coffin.

senet

A board game played by ancient Egyptians. It involved two players each with seven pieces and was played on a rectangular board divided into thirty squares. Archaeologists have found many senet boards in tombs, but haven't been able to work out what the rules of the game were.

stele (plural stelae)

A slab of stone or wood with an inscription or painting on it used in funerals. The stele had prayers to the gods on them, often mentioning all the offerings and worship that the dead person had given to the gods when he or she was alive.

underworld, afterlife

The ancient Egyptians believed that the earth was a flat disc. Beneath the earth was the underworld, a dangerous place. After they died Egyptians believed they had to first pass through the underworld before they could live forever in the afterlife.

vizier

A very important person. He was the pharaoh's chief minister. He made sure that Egypt was run exactly the way the pharaoh wanted it.

Look out for Ramose's further adventures in

Ramose, Prince of Egypt,
ASCENT TO THE SUN

ISBN 978-1-84647-42-4

Ramose may be a royal prince
but he's fighting for his life!

The world believes Prince Ramose is dead.
But he has been in hiding, living in
disguise, until he can resume his rightful
place as Pharaoh's heir. Now his biggest
test is still to come – and it seems the
gods have deserted him.

'Excellent thrillers...strong on incidental
details of Ancient Egyptian life...the
tension never flags as Ramose battles
for his rightful place against priests and
members of his own family'
Amanda Craig, *The Times*

Here is a short extract from the third story
in the series *Sting of the Scorpion*
(published in *Ascent to the Sun*)

NIGHT IN THE DESERT

"POOR MERY is hungry," said Karoya, stroking her cat. She threw the last pat of donkey dung on the spluttering fire. "She shouldn't be cold as well." The sandy-coloured cat sat as close to the flames as she could without burning her fur.

"We're all hungry," said Hapu grumpily. "But you're more concerned about that cat than us."

"We chose to be here. She didn't," said Karoya.

"Well, if we were travelling along the river we wouldn't be hungry," grumbled Hapu. "We could fish every day."

Ramose's stomach growled. Like the others he had eaten nothing but stale bread and dried figs for the last three days.

"We can't go back to the river, Hapu," said Ramose. "It's too dangerous."

Three days earlier, Ramose had seen men searching the riverbank. He was sure it was the vizier's men looking for them.

"We crossed over the river so that they couldn't find us," complained Hapu. "I don't see why we have to travel in the desert as well."

Ramose had insisted that they leave the fertile Nile Valley and walk parallel to the river but out of sight of the fertile land.

"We attract too much attention," Ramose said. "In Egypt everyone has a job to do, a place to be. Three young people shouldn't be wandering around the country by themselves."

Hapu grunted. He knew Ramose was right.

Ramose stared moodily into the fire. The flames were dying. A handful of reeds and a pat of donkey dung didn't burn for long. He saw a slight movement out of the corner of his eye. As he watched, a pale, creamy coloured scorpion crawled out from under a rock. It was big—more than a palm-width long. It climbed onto the rock and raised its pincers. Its tail curled menacingly above it. Ramose was about to reach out and squash it with his sandal. Then he realised that the creature was warming itself by the fire just as they were. He left it alone.

It was a strange situation for a prince to be in, travelling on foot, hiding in the desert, living like a barbarian. There was a reason why he was doing it though—a good reason. He was going back to the royal palace at Thebes. He had to let his father know that he was still alive. Then he would reclaim his place as Pharaoh's elder son and heir to the throne of Egypt.

It was over a year since one of his father's lesser wives had tried to poison him so that her own son, Tuthmosis, could become pharaoh. Ramose's tutor and nanny had saved him by pretending that he had died. They had hidden him in the tomb makers' village where he lived, as a scribe, for many months.

Karoya was roasting a snake over the tiny fire. That was to be their evening meal.

"I don't see why anybody would choose to live out here," grumbled Hapu. "Why didn't your people live in villages?" he asked Karoya. "Were they running away from someone?"

"No," said Karoya indignantly. "It was the life they chose."

Karoya was the only one who liked travelling close to the desert. It reminded her of her home in Kush, a desert country to the south of Egypt, which had been conquered during Pharaoh's last military campaign.

"But how did you survive?"

"My people knew the desert as well as Egyptians know the river. We kept herds of cattle. We were always moving, seeking grass for the cattle to eat. It was a good life."

Karoya was speaking as if her people didn't exist any more. Ramose knew that she had been captured by his father's army and forced to become a slave. He had never asked her what had happened to her family. He was afraid that the answer would make him ashamed of being Egyptian.

Karoya handed them each a piece of the snake and a gourd of water.

"It's like eating leather," grumbled Hapu, spitting out bits of snakeskin.

The snake was tough and tasteless, but Ramose didn't complain.

He glanced over at the black-skinned slave girl sitting next to him. Without Karoya's knowledge of the desert, Ramose knew they would have died of hunger. Their food supplies had been scanty, but what little they had, Karoya found. She had killed the snake. She had trapped a bird. She organised night-time trips back into the fringes of the cultivated land to collect water, grain and vegetables. Ramose didn't like adding to his crimes by stealing from people's fields and orchards. But they had no choice. He hoped Maat, the goddess of justice, would understand. He promised himself he would make an offering to her as soon as he could.

Hapu didn't know anything about the desert, but he was a loyal friend and good company. He told stories as they walked. Even when Ramose was feeling like he'd never achieve his goal, Hapu could always make him smile. Without his friends, Ramose may well have given up in despair.

"It's your turn to go and get water," Karoya said to Ramose.

Ramose nodded. He no longer thought it strange that a prince should do as a slave girl told him. Back in the palace, servants weren't even allowed to look him in the eye, let alone tell him what to do.

He took the water-skin and walked towards the fertile land. Thoth, the moon god, hadn't risen yet, but Ramose used the stars to guide him. It took him an hour to reach the first fields of the cultivated land. He found an irrigation canal surrounding a field of beans. He filled the water-skin and picked some beans as well.

By the time he got back to the camp, his friends were asleep. They had arranged their reed mats around the little fireplace—even though the fire had gone out. Karoya was wrapped in the length of faded cloth that she wore over her head. She was curled around Mery for extra warmth. Hapu only had a coarse linen shirt. Ramose wrapped himself in the woollen cloak that had been with him ever since he left the palace. It wasn't enough to keep out the cold of the desert night.

Two hours later, Ramose was still awake. The sand was as hard as a block of stone. He turned onto his back and stared up at the night sky. The stars in their millions twinkled above him.

In his head, Ramose ran through the events of the past weeks again and again. If he'd done things differently they wouldn't be in such a miserable state. A month ago, a high priest had accused them of being tomb robbers and tried to arrest them. They could easily have been imprisoned in Memphis. They'd had a narrow escape.

A wave of shame and anger crept over Ramose. The truth was, he was a tomb robber. He had stolen gold and jewels from Pharaoh Senusret's pyramid. It was the worst crime in Egypt and he was guilty of it. It hadn't been Ramose's choice, though. A gang of tomb robbers had kidnapped him and they had forced him to crawl into the heart of the pyramid and steal the gold and jewels from the tomb. Hapu had fallen into their clutches as well. The two boys had been abandoned, trapped underground. Mery had saved them. The cat had led them out of the tomb.

He was sure Vizier Wersu was pursuing them because they were tomb robbers. The vizier didn't know it was Ramose who had robbed the tomb. He, like everyone else, thought that Ramose was dead. That was the way Ramose wanted it to stay.

Ramose removed a sharp stone from under his back. He sighed and turned on his other side. He felt something prick his leg. He shifted again with annoyance. Would he ever get to sleep?

As he lay there, a swarm of mosquitoes suddenly attacked him. He couldn't see them, but he could feel them biting him all over. Then a tall, thin man with a face like a crocodile appeared from nowhere. He had his long, white robes draped over one arm as he walked. Even in the darkness, Ramose knew who it was. It was Vizier Wersu. He was holding a bronze statue of Seth in the form of a strange animal with square ears, a pointed snout and a forked tail. Seth was the god of chaos and confusion who had killed his own brother, Osiris, and gouged out the eye of his nephew, Horus, god of the sky.

Seth was an ugly-looking god, but the statue was a beautiful thing. Ramose thought about the cost of such a large bronze statue. It was probably enough to feed three families for a year. He wondered why anyone would want to worship such an unpleasant god. He admired the delicately carved hippopotamuses around the base. It's strange how you can see so much detail in dreams, thought Ramose. And odd how you can feel as well as see. He scratched furiously at the itchy bites all over his body.

The vizier had an evil look in his eye. He took hold of the feet of Seth with both hands and swung the statue as if it were a weapon. It was a weapon. He swung the heavy bronze statue again, aiming it right at Ramose. Ramose rolled out of the way and the statue dug into the sand, narrowly missing his head. He was surprised at the skinny vizier's strength. The vizier raised the statue above his head. Ramose tried to roll out of the way, but he caught his foot in his bag. Vizier Wersu brought down the statue hard on his right leg. It hurt. Ramose cried out in pain.

Then Ramose saw that in his other hand, the vizier held a large fig, the biggest fig Ramose had ever seen. Wersu was trying to force it into Ramose's mouth. Ramose tried to stop him, but he couldn't move because his leg was hurting and his body was itching from the mosquito bites. Wersu hit his leg again with the bronze statue. The pain was terrible. Ramose opened his mouth to scream and the vizier prised open Ramose's jaws and forced the fig in. The huge fruit wedged in his mouth so that he could neither spit it out nor swallow it.

It was cold, so cold. Ramose shivered and shivered and couldn't stop. He felt sick. This is a dream, he told himself. All I have to do is wake up. His eyes were wide open but he couldn't wake up.

The moon god, Thoth, finally climbed into the sky. Ramose was pleased to see the bright disc of the moon. Thoth was also the ibis-headed god of writing, worshipped by scribes. Thoth was only there for a moment before the black sky turned dark orange. The first rays of the sun were appearing over the horizon. Before long the sky was light and the moon faded until it was like a ghost of itself in the morning sky.

Karoya awoke and sat up. Hapu stirred in his sleep. Ramose realised with a jolt that he wasn't dreaming. He was awake. The pain in his leg from Wersu's blow was unbearable. The itching hadn't gone away. And try as he might, he could not swallow the fig jammed into his mouth. He tried to speak to Karoya, but he could only make a terrible animal noise.

Karoya knelt down at his side. Her forehead was creased with concern. She seemed to be shuddering and quivering from side to side. Then Ramose realised that it was him that was moving. He was shivering violently and couldn't stop.

"Hapu," said Karoya. "Quick, get the water."

Hapu sat up sleepily. As soon as he saw Ramose he jumped to his feet.

"What's happened to him?"

"I don't know, but he needs water. His tongue is so swollen, it looks like he might choke."

What's wrong with me? Ramose wanted to ask as he gulped the water, but he couldn't. He had never felt so sick. He was sweating as if he were lying out in the midday sun, but the sun's rays hadn't yet reached their camp. He couldn't breathe properly. He sucked in gulps of air. His heart was pounding. Karoya was swimming blurredly in front of him.

Ramose felt her hands as she searched his body for signs of injury or illness. She touched his right leg and he cried out in pain.

"Here," said Karoya. "Look. Something has bitten him."

Karoya pulled the cloak away from him. Ramose raised his heavy head and glimpsed his lower leg, which was swollen to the size of a melon. He might have imagined the vizier hitting him with a statue, but the pain was real.

Karoya suddenly snatched up her grinding stone. Ramose flinched as she held it above her head ready to hurl at him. He tried to cry out again. Not you, Karoya. You haven't turned against me, have you? No sound came out, but saliva dribbled from his mouth as if he were a baby. He felt a rush of air as the stone narrowly missed his leg and dug into the sand next to him. What is happening? he wanted to ask. Ramose felt his eyelids droop. His life was in danger, he didn't know what was real and what wasn't, but all he wanted to do was sleep. Karoya knelt down and picked up something very cautiously between her fingers. Ramose's vision was blurry, but he could make out what it was. It was a dead scorpion.